Spanking Tales
VOLUME II

AN EROTIC SHORT STORY ANTHOLOGY

EMILY ROOKS

True Lust

Contents

Harley

You're a schoolteacher, you can stop this. That's what I tell myself, as I move quickly toward the two boys circling one another, all while a crowd grows around them. I press my way through the gathering students, step directly between the two boys. A withered red leaf flutters down from a nearby tree. "There's a better way of solving this, isn't there, boys?" I say, my voice firm. Eleven-year-old freckled Tommy Bierderer sneers but remains otherwise still. "Well?" I say to Lindy as turning to him.

"Yes, ma'am," Lindy says.

"And what is that way?"

"We could talk through it."

"That's right." I look at Tommy. "Would you be willing to talk about this?"

"No," he hisses.

I cross my arms, tap my foot, and stare at him.

"But he–"

"I'm sure your grievances are real," I say, "but so are Lindy's. You're not going to plead your cases to me but instead work it out between the two of you. Do you understand?"

Tommy's hands ball into fists, then relax. "Okay," he mumbles.

"You two will discuss this with the counselor after recess," I say. "Right now, you are to stay apart from one another." I point to the west side of the playground. "Lindy, you will go to that side of the playground. Tommy, you will stay in the section with the swings." I point to the east. "Understand?"

"But I want to play on the swings–" Lindy starts, and I shoot him a *don't you dare* look. He skulks toward the tetherball pole.

Tommy chuckles, knowing he's won a small victory over Lindy. The rest of the children slowly peel off from the group, most voicing their disappointment amid speculations of who would have won the fight.

The truth, though, is *I* won.

I head back toward the school door, where I have a broader view of the playground.

"Nicely done, Marisa," the other playground monitor says. "You sure were in control."

I grin. *Control* is what it's all about.

***

A steady stream of single mothers, stepdads and stepmoms, and even the occasional biological mom and dad keep me busy that night at parent-teacher conferences. As the evening nears its end, only two students' parents haven't shown – Amelia Lewis's, who needed to reschedule due to a work conflict – and Tommy Bierderer's. Not that I expect Tommy's parents to show; parents of kids like him rarely do. I start to pack up for the day.

Footsteps sound at the door. I look up.

My breath catches, as a warming flush creeps up my neck. A mountain of a man stands in the doorway. He's at least six-foot-three, and muscles bulge from every part of his body. His black hair is slicked back, and his eyes are the most captivating hue of gray I've ever seen.

"I'm Dominic Bierderer, Tommy's father," he says and extends his hand.

This is Tommy's dad?

We shake hands, and a small tremor ripples through my body. *Self-control, Marisa, self-control,* I tell myself and stand straighter. I gesture to the small chair, made even smaller by his large body, as he sits in it. "I'm glad you were able to come this evening," I said. "I must admit, I didn't think that I'd see you tonight."

He pays my comment no attention. "Tommy likes you as a teacher. Says you're kind to him."

My chest tightens, and I glance at the floor tiles; to think, I've looked down on Tommy all this time. "I enjoy having your son as a student. I think he could do better, though; he just needs to apply himself more."

He nods. "I never liked school much, so I'm afraid I'm not much for helping him."

"So long as you encourage him, Mr. Bierderer, that alone will do wonders."

"Dominic. Call me Dominic, Miss Spencer. *Mr. Bierderer* makes me sound like a principal."

I giggle. "And Marisa is fine rather than Miss Spencer." *Wait, what did I just say?*

"My concern is that he passes," Tommy's dad says. "He almost didn't make it to this grade." His voice is

3

deep.

"Would he be willing to receive some extra help, maybe some tutoring? I'm here after school each night."

Dominic scratches his head, as if in thought. "Not sure that he would be up for staying after school. Do you think it would help?"

"If he's willing to put in the effort, it will. I'm confident we can get him caught up."

He sits there for a long moment, as if pondering something. "I'll talk to him about it, see what he'd like to do."

I push Tommy's report card across the children's table to him. He holds the sheet down, as I go through it subject by subject. As I point at Tommy's reading grade, I realize how small my hands are next to Dominic's bear paws.

After we finish, he stands. "I'll talk to him. As I said, he likes you, so he might be willing."

I rise as well. "It was a pleasure meeting you." I hold out my hand to shake his.

"The pleasure was all mine," Dominic says and takes my hand. My nipples tighten into tiny rosebuds.

As he leaves. I keep my eyes on the back of his head rather than let them stray to his ass, because that would be inappropriate.

Control is what it's all about.

***

As I reheat some leftovers for a late dinner that evening, I can't stop thinking about Dominic. His alluring gray eyes. Those massive hands. I stare out the window, watch the wind shake the withering leaves off the oak tree. Wisconsin's cold winter appears to be making an early arrival. Would be nice to have Dominic's warm body holding me through the night. The microwave *dings*. Well, any man's warm body really.

I sit down to eat the booyah. The stew tastes a bit flat...flat like my life. What was it my father always told me when I was growing up? *The more control you have, the better off you will be.* Hmpff. There were men back in college, but I held out on any long relationships until I found a job; I wasn't about to compromise my career and womanhood just so we could move to where some guy wanted to work. Unfortunately, small towns don't have much in the way of available men, not unless you count the drunks and those missing more teeth than they have. Just hang in there, I told myself through the years, someone will come along.

I just didn't expect it be someone like Tommy Bierderer's dad.

Dumping the remaining stew into the trash bin, I remind myself that someone *can't* be Dominic. We're totally wrong for another. This is just a crush born of desperation.

***

Twelve years ago...

The car radio plays Kanye's *Mercy* as Easton and I entwine our tongues and arms around one another. Our heat has long ago steamed up the windows that September night on some road that already was off of some country road following the home football game. Eventually our hands find the spots we are looking for – he my breasts and me his back, to keep him near.

He caresses the bare skin that my bra does not cover, and the spot between my legs tingles. His thumb brushes over a nipple, and I kiss him more deeply, as my heart picks up. He notices the effect, and his fingers play with my nipples, alternately rubbing and lightly pinching them. A wet spot forms on the front of my panties.

Then one of his hands runs along my waist and to the bottom of my back. It slips under my ass, squeezes a cheek. A soft moan escapes me. I wonder if he might slap it.

And then, as his lips skim along the side of my neck, I think back to being five, in kindergarten, when I first heard the word *spanking*. My friend Hallie had received one for being naughty. Though Hallie explained it as if it were something to avoid, I found myself intrigued, wondering what it felt like. Every time someone mentioned a spanking through elementary school, I found myself listening too closely.

And I always was ashamed of that.

Each time, I thought of what my father had told me in so many words during hot dish dinners and car drives to school and pep talks over lost boyfriends: Self-control is proof of maturity…The more self-control, the more you will be able to control others and so protect yourself…The more control you have, the better your life will be.

As *Mercy* reaches its last verse, my face turns red, and my body contracts in on itself. The idea that Easton's hand is squished between the car seat and my tush, so there is no way he could slap either, never crosses my mind, and I push him away.

Easton avoids looking at me, as he drives back onto the main road, back toward civilization. I remain silent, looking out the window into the blackness.

Who I am is woven from the fabric of *control*, I tell myself, as we pass silhouettes of farmhouses in the moonlight. Life is no more than a walk through a field of thorns, each one threatening to catch and rip that fabric. My strange fascination with spanking is one such thorn that I constantly have to sidestep.

Easton never asks me out again.

***

The next day after school, long after the last kids have left the building, Dominic appears at the classroom door. A white T-shirt hugs his broad shoulder and taut chest. I catch myself unconsciously reaching for my ass, to rub it, but stop myself just in time.

"I'm running errands on my day off and thought I'd stop in about Tommy staying after school," he says.

It's his day off? Well, that explains Tommy, he's unparented on weekends. "Come in Mr. Bier-, um, Dominic."

He steps toward my desk, and a woodsy, spicy scent wafts toward me. Is he wearing cologne? "Tommy says he's okay with meeting after school. Can you start tomorrow night?"

I pause a moment, surprised that Tommy was willing to get the extra help. *Never underestimate a student,* I remind myself. "Yes, we can. We'll need some ground rules first."

"Ground rules?"

"The extra time is meant for learning not socializing. I'll expect him to be here and in his seat five minutes after class. That will give him an opportunity to take a break and–"

Dominic scratched his head. "Tommy isn't much of one for rules. He's a free spirt. Guess he gets that from me."

"We'll need to have some rules if these afterschool sessions are to be productive."

"I'll let you work that out with Tommy."

No wonder Tommy has such poor self-control with the lack of parental involvement in his education, I tell myself. "There are rules for everything, Dominic."

He nods. "I understand. One of the reasons I didn't do well in school is because I had teachers who were control freaks. They had *too many* rules. I felt strangled in that kind of environment. Tommy might feel the same way." His gray eyes almost look like they are pleading with me.

"Well...okay. I'll approach Tommy with a gentle hand then."

"I appreciate that, Marisa. And I think you'll find with that approach *you* will appreciate it as well. Thank you for your time and helping Tommy."

With that, he walks out of my classroom, leaving me

something to ponder.

***

I brush my long hair in the mirror as getting ready for bed. I can't believe I almost touched my ass in front of Dominic. I can't believe all I have thought about since seeing him again was what a spanking from him would be like. Holding the hair brush in my hand, I find myself wondering if he would use it or his large hands.

Quick stuffing the brush into the drawer, I head to bed and crawl under the covers. *My big empty bed. What's wrong with me? Why am I thinking about being humiliated? I'm a strong woman.*

I close my eyes, trace my breast with a finger.

Still, there's no harm in pretending that we're together, for just a little while.

My hand goes between my legs, as my finger slowly runs up and down my cleft. I imagine it's Dominic's large hands, as he kisses the nape of my neck. Running a finger along the outside of the folds, I realize I'm already wet. It slips between the folds, flicks my clit, and my neck arches; it becomes Dominic's tongue down there, pleasing me.

Moments later, my hips gyrate to his tongue's ministrations, and my free hand caresses a breast then other one. I'm surprised to find that my nipples already are hard. Dominic's tongue works its magic as my breathing deepens. I groan in pleasure.

My neck arches further back, and I bite my lower lip. My body seems to rise. I moan, and as every muscle tenses, his large hand grips my leg, pulls it up so my ass rises off the bed. His free hand slaps it.

"Ohhhh!"

My hips buck up, and I let go a long, loud moan of pleasure. My body hovers on a current of warm air, as every part of my being relaxes. Then it floats back to the bed and settles softly upon the mattress.

That should keep me warm through the night.

***

I glance at the clock, see I've spent five more minutes with Tommy than planned. "Let's call it a night," I say. "You did a good job this afternoon."

He smiles then stuffs the math textbook into his desk. "See you tomorrow, Miss Spencer."

"Night Tommy."

I glance out the window. A cold gust lifts the leafless oak's branches, as darkness begins to settle. Hopefully the leftover stew will warm me tonight. Throwing on my coat and scarf, I head into the hallway. At the far end, two married teachers hold hands as they walk out of the building for an evening together at home. No, the stew won't be enough.

My blue mood almost turns black when the car doesn't start the first time I turn the ignition. It catches the second time, though, and I'm off.

No more than a couple of blocks from the school, I pass Tommy. He's coatless and walking with his head into the wind.

I pull off to the side of the street, wait for him to reach me and roll down the passenger window.

"Tommy?"

He looks my way. "Miss Spencer?"

"Tommy, where's your coat?"

He shrugs and looks away.

"Get in, I'll give you a ride home." I unlock the door.

Tommy hesitates a moment then jumps in.

"Buckle up, Tommy. I'll need directions."

He nods then shivers.

I'm going to have to find a way to get him some winter clothes.

***

Ten years ago...

Even though I've fantasized about getting spanked, the pain comes as a surprise.

My hands grip Tucker's ankles, as his strong hand holds my torso against his lap. We'd been play wrestling in his dorm room, and somehow I ended over his knees, where he promised to give me the spanking I'd always deserved. After a couple of swats, he pulls down my jeans and panties. I'm too red-faced – and too curious – to say anything.

His free hand whacks me hard. I squeal as the burn runs across my bare butt cheek. That handprint was going to stick around a while.

Am I victim of violence, I ask myself as he continues to render my "punishment." To violate someone is to rip away their control, and right now I haven't got much of a say.

If so, then why was I getting wetter?

I grind my pussy against his legs, feel my clit growing.

"I think you're enjoying this too much," he says, and

his body stretches for something. "Well enjoy *this*."

He whaps my full ass with the face of his table tennis paddle. *Like, whoa, shit, that does actually hurt a lot.* And then my whole body spasms as I let go a moan of pure pleasure and find myself floating. When I come down from the orgasm, Tucker gently lifts me off his knees, and his eyes look over me, as if searching for answers.

***

A couple of weeks pass, and Tommy is starting to catch up on his assignments. He seems more relaxed in class, less sullen and unfriendly to the other students.

"All tight, time to pack up, Tommy," I tell him. "Your father should be here any moment."

As if right on cue, Dominic steps into the classroom, and at the sight of him, my breath almost catches. Wednesdays are his day off, and I've found myself looking forward to that date.

"Hey Dad," Tommy says.

Dominic nods to him. "Tommy."

His son heads into the hallway, I presume to put on his winter clothes.

Dominic steps up to my desk, pulls a black wallet from his back pocket. "I need to pay you back for the coat, gloves and stocking cap you got Tommy."

"There's no need for that, Dominic."

"I can't accept that."

"And I can't accept the money, on principle."

He gazes at me for a long moment, maybe trying to comprehend why someone would be kind to him or Tommy. His free hand runs through his dark hair,

12

slightly raising his white T-shirt, and I catch a glimpse of his toned and tan stomach. He's underdressed, too, for the weather.

"I don't like to be beholden to anyone," he says at last.

"There are other ways than money to pay back someone."

Dominic pauses a moment, and his beautiful gray eyes lock onto mine. He stuffs his wallet back into his back pocket. "I like your necklace," he says at last. "It's very...becoming of you."

My hand goes to the necklace. It's a faux gold shell in the shaped of a heart. "Thank you."

He nods. "Tommy and I best be going."

With that, he walks out of the classroom, and I watch his pert ass the entire way.

***

Eight years ago...

I'm lying on my bed, but in my mind, I'm on all fours, my ass up in the air. In both reality and fantasy, a finger circles my clit. He's slapping my butt cheeks, shooting pulses of pain through me even as my finger's ministrations send waves of pleasure across me. Suddenly, the whole world around me – the noise of a passing car, the scent of my balsam and fir candle – fades and all that exists is the dream: the hand coming down fast toward my bare ass; the *whack* as skin slapping skin echoes off the walls; the scalding pain. I have total control of myself. Muscles tense then spasm as a soft, warm ecstasy overtakes me.

As my breathing calms and I hear a truck pass on the

street, my mind turns on me. *Am I really in control? I can't orgasm unless I fantasize about being spanked. The fantasy holds me hostage.*

I am powerless against this fantasy. It is a force that robs me of the very pleasure it brings.

I turn over and cry.

***

The next Wednesday, Tommy is absent from school. *Too bad,* I think, *we were making good progress, and now we have a whole day of work to make up. It also means not seeing Dominic for another week.*

As I'm packing my messenger bag, I hear a footstep at the door.

My heart thumps. *It's him.*

"I just wanted to apologize for Tommy not being here today," Dominic says. "He's ill."

"I hope everything is all right."

"Just the flu. I had to cover part of a shift for a co-worker who's also ill, so Tommy is at his aunt's."

Should I give him Tommy's homework, I ponder. *No, he won't be up to doing it if he's ill.* "The flu is going around. Hopefully he'll be back on his feet tomorrow."

Dominic nods. "I've been thinking about the clothing you got for Tommy, and how you said there were other ways than money to pay back someone."

I don't say anything, just gaze at him. Damn, his narrow and angular, sharp jawline are sexy as hell. And those gray eyes...

"Perhaps I could take you out to dinner on Friday. Tommy's aunt is having a sleepover for her boys, and he

14

will be there."

I fidget a moment. For as good looking as Dominic is, I'm uncertain if I should be dating a student's parent. Well, it's not a date, just a dinner to show his appreciation for something I did outside of school business.

"I'd like that," I say, and he smiles.

***

Five years ago...

For months, I try not to think about being spanked while attempting to orgasm. It all comes to no good, and my body feels tight, stiff, not having enjoyed a release in so long.

Then I figure it out, on the playground of all places.

There's a commotion at the monkey bars. Looks like it involves Gabe, this year's behavioral problem poster child. I head over there, watch three kids shove him, and he pushes back with all kinds of hollering going on.

"Everybody stop!" I shout a few feet from them. "What's going on here?"

"Gabe keeps cutting the line!" one boy says, and his two companions vocally second his assertion.

"Is that true, Gabe?"

He glares at the ground with pursed lips. "They're too slow! I just stand around waiting for them!"

The other three argue back.

"Everyone quiet down! Pushing one another on the playground is dangerous. Someone could get hurt if they hit the monkey bars or fell. Here's what we're going to do. Gabe, you will let Barry, Jim and Ted go first. You can stand by the front of the monkey bars, and after one of them climbs up, you say 'Your turn!' to the next in line. After Ted goes, you say 'My turn!' and go. Does everyone understand?"

All of them nod.

"Let's try it."

They run through it with flying colors. Gabe has something to keep himself busy and doesn't cut. When he starts smiling, I head back to my watchful position next to the playground monitor.

"How do you do it, Marisa?" she says.

"It's all about the *illusion of control*. Gabe thinks he's in charge of the monkey bars. The reality is he's just following playground rules by waiting his turn."

"Sure glad you weren't my mother," she says. "You would have convinced me to enjoy folding laundry rather than going out on Saturday nights."

We laugh, and that's when it came to me: What I'm looking for is the illusion of the *loss* of control. When fantasizing about spanking, I'm not truly submitting to this kink or to the man spanking me. The fantasy is *mine*; I am not at its mercy. I am in control even as I feel like I've suddenly lost it.

That evening, I masturbate as fantasizing about Tucker spanking me with his table tennis paddle and cum after just a few imagined whacks. I've never felt so powerful – or slept so well – as that night.

***

After school that Friday, I drive to the Red Barn Café on the outskirts of town to meet Dominic. Unseasonably warm, a temporarily break in winter's inevitable march, I leave my jacket in the car and straighten my blouse before going inside.

At a table near the back, Dominic waves at me. His large hands look normal size to me from that distance. I wonder what it would be like to have one of those large hands swat my little tush. Putting on a smile, I walk slowly toward him.

"Hope you don't mind me getting a table for us," he says as I get close.

"Not at all." I take the chair across from him.

"Thanks for joining me. More importantly, thank you for helping Tommy. It's not often that people are kind to him."

Am I being more kind to Tommy than other students, I wonder, letting my feelings for Dominic cloud my judgment? Wait, *feelings for Dominic?* Yes, I find him attractive, but I don't have any feelings for him.

"He's a good boy who just needs to apply himself," I say. "Once he's caught up, he can do just as well as the other students if he chooses to remain caught up."

"You mean if he shows a little self-discipline?"

That probably is a sore subject for Dominic. "I'm just saying he's quite capable of succeeding academically."

Dominic nods. "There's always a value in knowing when to let go."

The waitress arrives, takes our orders. We both know what we want without having to crack open the menu.

When she leaves, I look at Dominic, admire that perfect jawline for a long moment. "You were saying

17

there's a value in knowing when to let go. What did you mean?"

"I like to be in charge, too, which probably is why my relationship with Tommy's mother was a little difficult at times. Tommy's like me... wants to be in charge of himself. Try to rein him in, and he just rebels more. Knowing when to stop reeling can go a long way."

"I'll keep that in mind with Tommy." *And should I keep that in mind with you, Dominic?* "To be honest, though, I have trouble...letting go."

Somehow being vulnerable in front of Dominic feels right.

He gazes at me for a few seconds, as if thinking of something. "Well, you know what they say about the easiest way to get straight A's in school."

I wait for the answer, and when he says nothing, with a smile I shrug.

"Use a ruler."

I break out in laughter. Cheesy joke, I know, but so true in a number of ways. I wonder a moment which would be better – to be spanked by his large hands or by him wielding a ruler?

"Oh Dominic, you're a good father."

Our meal arrives, and the conversation settles into less significant topics.

***

Three years ago...

For two weeks, Jason and I sit next to one another in the teacher's lounge during our free hour, laughing and joking. Somehow we find excuses to visit the other's classroom before or after school, and should I see him down the hallway, my eyes are sure to follow.

At last the moment arrives. Jason, his shoulders broad and torso V-shaped, stops in after school, just before all the teachers are to leave for the day, and looks me in the eye.

"Marisa, would you go out to dinner with me tomorrow night?" he says. "I was thinking the Aline and Dine, if only for our privacy."

Ah, the supper club near the neighboring town of Aline. He'd thought this through.

And for me, an opportunity to finally not be alone. Yet...

I look away, my heart breaking. I've spent years of limiting myself to fantasy. In those reveries, I can be in control... and the man of my desires never leaves me.

At that moment, I realize the real reason I won't find a guy is because I can't bear to lose him when I tell him of my kink. In reality, control isn't always guaranteed.

And Jason is too nice of a man to lose.

Better to not have him at all.

I look back to him. "I'm sorry, Jason, I just want to remain friends."

His face seems to sink in defeat, and he suddenly looks like he's aged 10 years in a second. "Okay," he says softly.

"But thank you, I'm very flattered." Small consolation.

We still talk but not as frequently. A year later, Jason and one of the newly hired teachers date and then marry, living out what we could have had.

***

Somehow dinner with Dominic turns into a two-hour conversation. Dominic talks about his road trips to Sturgis, how Tommy's mother died in a car accident when he was just an infant. He proves to be a good listener, too, despite that my stories about how I decided to go into elementary education and my vague answer to his question about why I wasn't married hardly measure up to his tales. *That's what happens when you're in control,* I tell myself, *you lead a safe, boring life. But that's a good thing, right?*

We walk out of the restaurant together into the dimming light. I shudder at the chilled air and wish for my jacket.

"Thank you for dinner," I say. "We're even now."

Dominic grins, tells me he enjoyed my company, and heads to his bike.

In my car, I turn the ignition, but only a sputtering sound follows. "Damn, not this again." I try once more but nothing.

Dominic appears at my driver's window, and I roll it down. "Car trouble?"

"I've been having problems starting it. Once I do, it runs just fine."

He nods. "Pop your hood…Try starting it now."

I turn the ignition, press the gas. A whirring sound then several clicks follow.

Dominic shuts the hood, leans at my window. "You need a new starter. I can get one for it tomorrow and fix it. I'll give you a ride home."

"On your bike?"

He nods again. "I'll need your car key once you lock up."

"I can't ask you to fix my car."

"Why not?"

"I'd be imposing on you."

"Not at all. I offered to fix it."

"Is a starter expensive?"

He shrugs. "I can find a used one that will be cheaper than buying new."

I lock my doors and hand him the car key. "I've never ridden a bike before."

"Just wrap your arms around my waist and lean into my back."

It was a nice bike, the kind of Harley that turns heads. He jumps on then tells me to climb up behind him. I do and hesitantly wrap my warms around his stomach, like he had told me. His woodsy, spicy scent fills my nostrils.

A moment later, the engine roars to life in a raw, guttural growl, and he looks over his shoulder at me. "Hold on tight."

The bike soars ahead, and my tummy suddenly lurches. It was like riding a Ferris wheel with only the seat for your butt – no safety bar, no sides, no back – and my head spins for a moment. I press my body into his and close my eyes.

We hit the highway, and our speed picks up. Despite the chill in the air, Dominic's body keeps me warm. A few moments later, as my stomach settles, I open my eyes, just out of curiosity. The evergreens and cuts

21

through the beige sandstone hills blur past us, as the wind whips through my hair.

And then I think, *this must be what a bird feels like when it flies.*

***

One year ago...

Envious of what Jason and his wife have, I accept Karson's invite to dinner. We work at different school buildings, met at a districtwide teacher in-service, and he is nice.

It progresses quickly, both of us eager to enjoy that American dream we were coming late to – marriage, a house, children. Too fast, apparently, because by the third date we sleep together...and then came all-weekend long sex marathons from Friday night through Sunday afternoon. The three-day weekends are the best. He doesn't seem to mind that I don't cum, a typical guy if truth be told, then one day he does.

Karson rolls onto his side, traces his finger along the curve of my hip as we recover from out latest session of coitus. "Is everything all right, honey?" he says.

"Sure. Why do you ask?" But I know why.

"It's just that...well..." His face blushes a bit.

I wait to speak, hoping he'll say it's nothing. He's a capable lover, even if for me orgasm remains out of reach each time we couple up. Somehow fantasizing about spanking doesn't work when actually having sex.

"Well...I don't think I've ever seen you cum," he says. "Don't I make you happy?"

Ah, it's about *him*. He doesn't think he's performing

22

well enough, and his masculinity is threatened. I ruffle the shock of black hair hanging over his forehead. "You make me very happy."

"But not in bed?"

"I keep jumping back into it with you, don't I?"

"Is there a reason you don't cum? Something I'm doing wrong?"

"You're doing just fine. I enjoy our sex."

His blue eyes narrow, as they always do when he's thinking. "Then is there something wr–...well, something *you're* having trouble with?"

He's dancing around it, trying not to accuse me of being messed up. Obviously if he's a red-blooded American male, I should naturally orgasm every time we have sex. The problem is, he's partially right...something is troubling me.

Should I tell him?

My lips part as I'm about to speak. But his unfinished word lingers in my mind – *Is there something wrong?*

"Women aren't like men. It takes time for us to feel comfortable enough to orgasm."

Karson stares at me, his upper lip slightly raised, his lower lip pushed up. It's his standard expression when he's doubtful. Women probably have cum the first time he's had sex with them, and we're up to what ... dozens of times?

"You don't feel comfortable with me then?" he finally says.

I touch his arm. "Of course I do, sweetheart." But that's a lie. If I was, I would have told him right then and there. And with that, I know our relationship days are numbered.

***

Late Saturday morning, my car rolls into my driveway. As I step outside into the warmth, Dominic rises from the car and says it's all fixed.

"Oh my God, really? How much do I owe you?"

He waves me off. "I'm paying you back for helping Tommy."

"You paid me back when you bought me dinner last night."

"With what little you ate, I didn't make a dent into what was owed."

I smile, maybe even blush a little.

"Well, you can pay me back by giving me a ride to the diner," he says, "so I can get my bike."

"That's more than fair."

When we get to the diner, Dominic turns to me. "Why don't you go riding with me today? The guy I covered for earlier this week is taking my shift, and Tommy will be at his aunt's all day. I planned to go up to Charlton Lake."

I gaze at the red, yellow and orange leaves on the maples and the perfectly clear blue sky, then remember the exhilaration of riding with him last night. "Okay, let's go."

Hopping on the bike behind Dominic, I wrap my arms around his waist, lean my body into his. The Harley takes off, and my stomach lurches again, though not as much as when he brought me home. Seconds later, we're on the highway, and as we leave town, Dominic picks up speeds up, going faster than my first bike ride.

The loud hum of his motorcycle as the road's white lines shoot toward then underneath us leave me dizzy, so I look off at the passing trees, streaks of red and gold and brown and orange and hunter green, interrupted by angled white fences and houses looking like parallelograms as we zip past them, all while Dominic's spicy cologne swirls around me. I wonder a moment if this is what being high is like.

No, not exactly, it's something else, for it's also about Dominic throwing caution to the wind – neither of us wears a helmet, there's no seatbelt, just me holding on to him for dear life...and me growing comfortable with that. It's a sense of freedom.

Never mind that the vibrations of the seat are working magic on my pussy.

***

High in the hills along some back country road out in the middle of nowhere, Dominic pulls the Harley into an overlook. I climb off, gaze at the valley below. It's a sea of amber, orange and burgundy leaves with a blue stream ribboning through it on the way to Charlton Lake.

Dominic walks up alongside me, wraps his large arm around my waist. I melt into his side, feel safe and warm.

I look up at him. "It's beautiful."

He tilts his head and slowly closes upon my face. I fill the gap. Our lips meet, soft and tender, lingering. Then he sucks on the cupid's bow of my upper lip for a second, and we return to kissing, his spicy scent leaving me heady. Pulling back for air, our eyes lock, and then we kiss again, unable to keep apart from one another. As his hands glide upon my back, he nibbles on my lower lip, just for a second or two, then our mouths meet again and open for one another. I massage his tongue then he mine, as we engage in a dance both primal and urgent.

I come up for air, my knees weak, but his strong arms hold me in place as his kisses trail from my mouth down the side of my neck. Gasping, my head arches, as I writhe from the sensations. I sense I'm losing control – but the freedom that comes with that loss is exhilarating.

My mind spins, as his warm lips find the nape of my neck. I need to gain control of my myself – and the only way to do that is to gain control of Dominic, to possess him.

As he kisses, I slowly grind against him, gyrating my hips in a circle. He lets go a moan into my skin, and then I feel a bulge growing beneath his denim. My grinding concentrates on it, and his member rises like mercury in a thermometer on a hot day. It is *me* who's doing this to him; it is *my* body that's driving him crazy. Dominic's hands drop down to my ass cheeks, push me against his full erection. I slide up and down it, teasing him.

At last he comes up for air, and I slink my body back from him, uncertain what might happen next.

***

"I know what you need," Dominic says, as we gaze into one another's eyes.

"Yeah, what's that?" I say breathily.

His large hands press my tiny tush forward, and he rubs his crotch up and down against mine. My toes curl.

"I need something else first," I whisper huskily.

His beautiful gray eyes seem to roll; he is probably thinking I want him to say he loves me. That would be nice, but it's not what I want, not yet anyway. I rake my fingers through his hair, and it is enough for him to say, "What would that be?"

"I want you to spank me."

His eyebrows rise, and he pulls back slightly. A long second passes, and his eyes fix on mine. He lets me go. "Pull down your pants and lean over the seat of my bike."

I walk over to the Harley, unsnap my jeans and wiggle them down to my ankles. Then I lean over his bike, resting my tummy on its seat.

"Your panties too."

I swallow hard then pull them down as well and bend over the bike again. He can see everything, including my wetness.

Stepping up behind me, he gazes down at me. I'm vulnerable and exposed. My belly twists and churns, as I think how much it is going to hurt.

Smack!

I screech "Aaaaiieeee!" as if a white hot plate had buried itself in my behind.

"Too bad I don't have a spanking paddle," he says.

"That would be appropriate given you're a teacher."

I giggle at that. "Your large hands are just fine."

Smack!

My ass writhes and clenches, as my pussy pulses.

"Perhaps I should use my belt."

I gulp. Wouldn't that hurt? I'd never tried it before.

Smack!

My butt cheeks twitch with heat, and I fight the instinct to reach a hand back to cover my ass.

"You are being quite naughty after all. I'd say that warrants more than a hand."

Smack!

A tiny gasp escapes my mouth. As my ass smolders, my pussy moistens.

Then I hear his belt buckle snap off and the slide of leather through the denim loops of his jeans. "I'm not sure why I'm asking you – after all, I'm the one in control here."

No, *I'm* the one allowing myself to be at your mercy. *I'm* in control.

SMACK!

His belt, folded into a loop, comes down across both of my ass cheeks, and I yelp. I press my tummy tight into his seat, bracing for the next strike.

SMACK!

My lower legs kick up, and he places his paw of a hand on my lower back to hold me in place. "Let's not knock my Harley down, all right?"

SMACK!

My leaking pussy grinds against the side of his

leather seat. Engorged, my clit pokes through the puffy cleft and finds leather. Suddenly, the whole world around me – the singing of the birds, the scent of the pine trees – fades and all that exists is the sound of Dominic's belt striking my ass and the exquisite, delightful burning that follows.

SMACK!

"I suspected from the day we met, Marisa, that you were the kind of woman who could only cum if she were spanked. It's that way with all control freaks."

SMACK!

I hold a fist to my eyes, as tears fall from the pain, all while waves of pleasure build deep inside me, each stroke against his leather seat slowly rippling outward, growing stronger and traveling farther than the last.

SMACK!

"Let me help you cum, Marisa."

Oh my God, what did he say? And then my whole body tenses, every muscle taut as a board, and I spasm as letting out a loud scream of pleasure.

Dominic tosses his belt to the ground, as I convulse, little aftershocks of the main orgasm. He spits on the burning strips across my ass then with his large hands rubs it into my skin, soothing the redness.

***

As I catch my breath, Dominic unbuttons his jeans behind me. I hear them puddle at his boots. A second later, the gravel beneath his feet shifts, and his cock is at my entrance. His large hands run through my long hair, separates it into two parts on the sides of my head like he was going to braid it into pig tails. Then his fists tighten across the two groups of hair and pulls them out and slightly back as his cock fills me.

I gasp. His cock is large, leaves no wiggle room as it touches every nerve in my pussy. My eyes close, as I bask in the sweet pleasure.

Then Dominic thrusts in and out of me with abandon, holding my hair, riding me as if I were his Harley. I grip his bike seat as my mouth widens, trying to bring in air at the same time that I let go ever louder murmurs. His speed picks up; he must have me.

His grunts and my moans echo across the valley. If anyone is down there hiking, they surely know that two people are fucking on top of this hill. That he doesn't care – that I no longer care – turns me on so much.

"You've got one tight pussy, Marisa," Dominic says, as his fists tighten their grip on my hair. "I'm not going to last long."

Waves of pleasure ripple again, growing each time his cock plunges into me.

He makes one last deep thrust and growls as his cum shoots deep inside my pussy. My walls clench his cock, as I spasm and scream in ecstasy. For a long moment, my body feels incredibly light, like a young bird taking to the sky for the first time.

***

Our fingers entwine, as he pulls me up off his Harley. I turn around to face him, but go too fast as my dizziness and weak knees cause me to collapse into his embrace. His cockhead brushes cum on my thigh, as my head presses into his chest.

"I see now what you mean about letting go," I say.

He caresses my back. His woodsy, spicy scent mixed with his sweat smells so good.

"You seemed hesitant at first to spank me."

"I was surprised. I didn't think you were ready to let go."

I thought back to my fantasies of Tucker spanking me, of turning down a really great guy in Jason, of not being to tell Karson why I couldn't cum, of all my lonely nights born out of fear. "How could you tell I was struggling?"

"Because I went through the same battle myself."

"With Tommy's mother," I say, recalling our conversation at the Red Barn Café.

He nods. "You're really only in control when you let go."

I snuggle my head against his chest. "Maybe you're the one who ought to be teaching school."

He chuckles.

And then we hear a car climbing the hill, its engine gaining in pitch as it approaches the crest and ultimately will pass us.

"You know that we're both standing here half naked," Dominic says.

Yeah, both of our asses hang out in the breeze. "Fuck it," I say, as wrapping my arms tighter around him. "Fuck it."

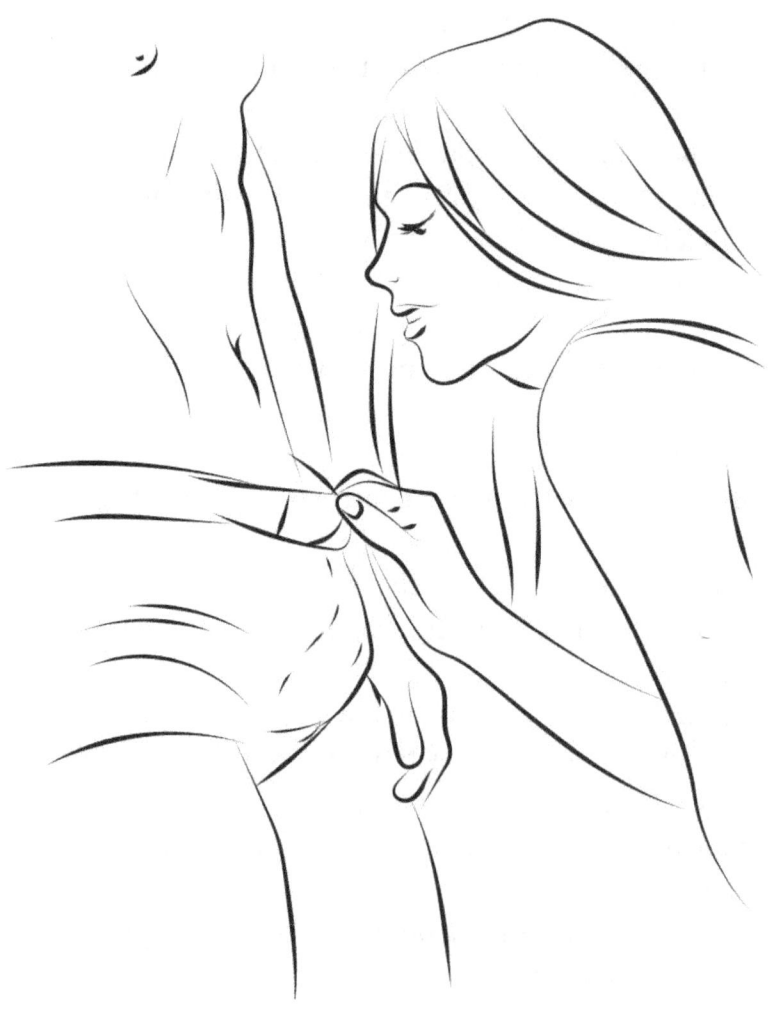

Lolly Hammer

The rain beats down on the plastic I've tacked up over the broad hole in my roof, drowning out the insurance agent on the phone. I do make out the words "unfortunately can't pay out on that."

"But how can that be?" I say. "I've made all of my payments on time."

"Roof damage isn't covered in your policy."

"Then just what the hell was I paying for all these years?"

"Your policy covers many things, such as the structure of your home, personal belongings within the home, and liability for accidents or injuries that occur on your property–"

"And a roof isn't part of the structure?"

"It is, but the structure itself – the beams that form the roof's shape – weren't damaged. This is just a hole between the beams."

"If the hole doesn't get fixed, there will be serious damage to the structure – and not just the roof but the floor and the walls that the water coming through the hole flood!"

"We wouldn't be able to cover that structural damage, as it occurred due to neglect since you failed to fix the hole in the roof."

"Oh Jesus Christ!" I disconnect and slam the cell phone against the counter.

The front door opens. "Kylie? Is everything all right?" It's Rochelle, my next door neighbor.

"Just arguing with my insurance agent."

"I was out walking and heard shouting. Just wanted to make sure everything was okay."

"It will be if I can find a way to pay for that." I point to the hole where plastic sags under the weight of pooling rain.

She nods, understanding in her eyes. "They do have a way of making you feel powerless, don't they? Tight for money?"

"Always. The curse of being a single parent."

"I might know someone who can fix that for you, and it won't cost you much at all. He's amenable to working out payment plans with clients."

Spending any money at all didn't sound good, but I was left with little choice unless I wanted my home to collapse. "That would be great. What's his name?"

"Jeremiah. Have you heard of him?"

I shook my head. "Should I have?"

Rochelle didn't say anything for a moment then pulled her phone from a back pocket. She scrolled through it. Here's his number."

I enter it into my phone. "Thanks. And thanks for checking on me."

"That's what neighbors are for – helping out one another."

I smile. "It is."

Rochelle leaves, and I tap Jeremiah's name in my contacts. Hopefully he can fix this before the Memphis heat gets horrendous. I can't imagine what my electric bill will be with that hole sucking out my AC this summer.

***

Two days later, Jeremiah stares up at the plastic-covered hole. He's not bad looking by any means – wavy black hair, piercing green eyes, smells vaguely of cedarwood – and I won't mind having him working around the house for a day or two. He might even provide some fodder for a fantasy session with my Magic Wand.

"Damaged during the storm?" he says, his voice deep and resonant.

"The one last Thursday."

He nods. "It damaged a lot of homes across Memphis. And insurance won't pay, you say?"

"They said the 'structure' of the roof wasn't damaged."

Jeremiah snorts. "What's really damaged is their moral compass."

"Finally, someone who sees things my way! So you can fix it?"

He nods. "Should take a day or two. I'll need to tear out the area damaged by the rain since the hole formed then put it all back together with new wood and roof tiles."

"How much?"

He says nothing for a moment. "The thing is, if you don't get it fixed, the rain is going to do further damage to your roof, the floor beneath it, and probably the walls. You live alone?"

That's an odd question. "Just me and my daughter."

"She's in school?"

Maybe he's going to give me a discount because of my dire straits. "She is."

He nods. "I'd have to be a selfish asshole to take advantage of you when you're in a situation like this."

Yes! The price will be low!

"How much did Rochelle tell you about me?" he says.

"Nothing really. Just that you were willing to work with clients who couldn't pay."

He grins. "I am. The issue always is *if* the client is willing to agree to my payment plan."

God, he's dragging this out. Why? "Just how much are you talking about?"

"Well, you see Kylie – you don't mind that I call you Kylie, do you?"

I shake my head.

"Well, you see I have no shortage of work coming my way. It keeps my busy – so busy that I don't have much of a social life. But a man – and a woman for that matter – can't spend their whole life only working. So when I come across someone who is short on money and a pretty lady like you are, I'm always willing to take payment in other ways."

My eyebrows rise. "Ohhhhh."

"But are you willing to pay...in *other* ways?"

My initial thought is *no*, but I'm curious just how much I'd have to give to get that roof fixed. "What would you want?"

"First we'll watch a movie together. While we do, you'll allow me to get you turned on."

Gee, he makes it sound like he's just looking out for my interests.

"Then you will let me eat your pussy. I love the taste of a woman. By the way, you'll first need to shave down there. I don't like hair between my teeth."

My mouth parts slightly, yet I find my mind betraying me, as I imagine his head between my legs, his wet tongue parting my cleft.

His green eyes drill into me. "After you cum, I will spank you. Over my knee."

My, he's confident – *after you cum*. Yet the idea of feeling a man's power overcoming my resistant mind, my resistant body, somehow sounds quite exciting.

"And lastly, I get to fuck you. By the way, I will cum in you as well. I won't have sex any other way."

I gulp. And risk a pregnancy?

Feeling a little snarky, I say, "In what position?"

"What is your favorite?"

I blush. "I don't think I exactly have one."

"Well, you think about it and let me know. As a matter of good faith, I will start the project by tearing out what needs to be replaced and will order the materials to finish the job. The second day when I come back, you'll pay me. The third day, I'll finish the roof. Do we have a deal?"

I stand there for a long moment, and can't believe what I say next. "Yes."

***

My daughter jumps into her chair, late again for breakfast. In her mind, she isn't. There is plenty of time to scarf down a bowl of cereal and whatever else I dish up. The light, floral scent of the neighbor's Rose of Sharon wafts through the open window, as I fill my daughter's glass with orange juice.

"Don't forget your raincoat," I tell her. "It's sunny now, but the weatherman says there may be thunderstorms this afternoon."

"Why can't you just pick me up if it rains?" she says between mouthfuls of Corn Flakes. "You're on vacation this week."

"I have a lot of cleaning to do." *And relaxing too – this is supposed to be my week off.*

"Mommy, can I go on the class field trip to Lululand?"

When I was kid, we took field trips to museums and farms. Today, kids get fun days to amusement centers if they're well behaved and have turned in all of their schoolwork. *How much will this cost me?*

"What day is the field trip?" I ask.

"Friday next week. It's $25."

I do some quick calculations to see how I can scrounge up the money.

She misinterprets my silence. "If you can't afford it because of the roof, I understand."

My heart breaks. I don't want to cheat her of the opportunity, of the experience, and since I don't have to pay for the roof and with saving on gas money this week because of vacation, I should be able to swing it.

I run my hand through her hair. "Don't you worry about that. Yes, you can go."

"Thanks Mommy!"

I smile at her, but then the thought crosses my mind – am I whoring myself out for my daughter?

***

I fidget as Jeremiah's truck pulls into the driveway about an hour after my daughter leaves for school. He grabs a toolbox and ladder from his pickup bed, and I tell myself to go out and stop him, to save him all this trouble. But I am too embarrassed. What if someone overhears?

When Jeremiah knocks on the door, I invite him in. Smiling, he carefully brings through the entry his aluminum ladder and a toolbox with a hammer sticking out from it.

"Jeremiah, before you go any further…"

He stops, waiting expectantly. His little boy's smile has got me doubting my decision.

"I can't go through with this."

He stares at me for a long moment. "I understand. It's no hard feelings. The payment arrangement isn't for everyone, and I respect that."

I don't know how the hell I'm going to get that roof fixed, but I'll find a way. "I'm sorry to have troubled you."

"There's no need to apologize, Kylie. Best of luck with everything."

He's right, I think, *why am I apologizing? I was trading sexual favors for a roof repair.*

Jeremiah heads back out the front door, just as careful as before, and puts everything in his truck. Then from his back pocket he whips out a smartphone and taps the screen. "Lynette? ... Good news, I can work on your roof today. Do you mind if I come on over? ... Excellent, I'll be there in just a minute; I am actually right across the street from you."

***

Through the day I listen to Jeremiah's electric saw cut wood out of Lynnette's roof and then a *thwump* on her lawn, as he tosses the debris. Sometimes I watch from behind a partially open curtain, standing back just far enough to see his pert butt yet not be seen myself. His muscled arms look so damn sexy, so commanding, when he swings his hammer.

There is no way I can pay for my daughter's fun day, as I need that roof repaired. I'm not sure how I am going to break it to her, especially after I just said she could go.

Seeing Jeremiah's sexy body working on that roof, a sudden desire to shower and masturbate overcomes me. I think about what he said he would do to my body – eat my pussy until I came...spank me over his knee...fuck me without a condom and cum inside me. That sounds better than any man I'd been with, even my ex-husband when we were at our randiest. Compared to what Jeremiah offered in return, I'd certainly given myself to men for much less – dinner and a movie, just treat me nice – all to satisfy my own urges.

I decide to approach him at day's end when he loads up his truck. My daughter is going on that field trip, damn it.

***

The setting sun casts a warm glow over the neighborhood as Jeremiah packs his truck with the tools of his trade. I cross the street to him, but he pays me no attention.

"Jeremiah," I say, and he looks my way. "I've been thinking about what I said this morning. I got afraid and made a hasty decision. I'm willing to agree to your payment arrangement after all."

He places his hands on his hips and gazes at me for a few seconds. "I'm still willing to fix your roof, Kylie, but my schedule is all filled up for the next few days. It would have to be next week sometime."

"Next week? But this is my vacation week, the only one I have off. And it's supposed to storm this weekend – I don't think my roof can handle another hard rain."

"Well, that's something you should have thought about this morning. I don't mean any disrespect, but what would I tell my other clients who are depending on me being there?"

My head drops. "I can't take time off of work next week to be home for you."

"In that case, I guess you'll need to pay someone to repair the roof."

With that, he gets into his truck and takes off, leaving me standing in the middle of the street. That asshole –

he's no better than the insurance company.

***

The next day, there's a knock on the door about mid-morning. It is Jeremiah. I open the door but don't let him in. The heat already is sweltering.

"I thought about it overnight," he says, "and I can talk my way out of the scheduled work if you're still interested. I get to choose the position, however. Consider it my bonus."

A bonus? What the fuck? My hands ball into fists. "You know, you make me feel like a whore that you're bartering for."

I slam the door in his face, storm into the kitchen. The dishes still need washing. I'll at least have clean plates in my flooded home.

Five minutes later, there's another knock.

I open it to see Jeremiah still standing there. Before I can scream at him to get off my property, he quick says, "Okay, *you* can decide the position. Frankly, Kylie, I've been thinking about you since we met Monday, and I'd be blessed to make love to you any way you would like."

I glare at him, trying not to let his boyish smile melt my reserve. "You can start today?"

"Right now, as a matter of fact, Kylie. I'll just need to come in for a few minutes to examine the underside of the roof again before I get started."

"Okay."

Jeremiah follows me, but as the door closes behind him, he grips my forearm. I spin around, and turned on by his power over my still resistant mind and body, I have this sudden urge to jump into his arms despite that he's grabbed me. Gazing into my eyes, he gently brushes a strand of hair out of my face. When his mouth closes on mine for a kiss, I meet him halfway. Our lips play against one another, deeply, passionately. He lets go of my arm, and an instant later my hands are on his head and his arms wrapped around my back.

We pull away from one another to catch our breaths.

"Let's save that for tomorrow," he says. "I've got a roof to get started on, and you've got a pussy to shave."

***

On Thursday morning, Jeremiah arrives right on time, an hour after my daughter left for school. I meet him at the door only wearing short shorts and a loose-fitting tee. This time Jeremiah doesn't carry his tool box or ladder but instead has his computer bag.

"I brought the movie for us to watch," he says.

"What's the title?" I ask. I hope it's a romance.

Jeremiah doesn't answer, just plugs his computer into my television then sits on the sofa. He takes off his work boots and socks, pats the space next to him.

I join him, and his arm snakes around me, pulls me closer. He points a remote at his laptop, and a moment later the movie begins.

The title comes on the screen – "Deep Tissue" starring Venus Gold. Great, he's brought a porno.

The movie opens with an hourglass-shaped blonde – I assume she's Venus Gold – entering a massage parlor and saying she's there to redeem the free massage she's won. Venus is a little surprised that she's actually won a free *naked* massage but undresses anyway. She even takes off her thong, though if she wore that to a massage, I suppose she doesn't mind being naked.

Venus gets on the massage table. Her muscular masseur comes in – he's only wearing shorts – and pours a liberal amount of oil all over her then kneads her back. He is doing a fairly good job, I admit; I could use a good back rub myself.

Through the scene, the tip of Jeremiah's finger grazes the length of my bare arm.

When the masseur caresses Venus' ass, Jeremiah's fingers reach my shoulder, kneads the muscles, light and gentle at first than more firmly, leaving me feeling utterly relaxed. My eyes start to glaze.

His other hand slowly, almost feather-like, runs the length of my thigh from the knee to the edge of my shorts then back again, goes a little higher the next time, then back up my thigh but a bit lower than at first. I want to tell him to go just a wee lower, and he'd find me cooing; he seems to read my mind and does just that on the return trip to my knee. I let go a low murmur, and he stays on that line from knee to shorts. On the way up, though, he doesn't stop at my shorts but keeps going, ending just before my pussy.

The masseur has Venus turn over so she's lying on her back. After some cursory work on her legs and arms, he focuses on her breasts and then the folds of her pussy. She moans.

Jeremiah's hand trails up my abdomen, caresses my breasts through the T-shirt, eliciting more murmurs. I didn't bother wearing a bra since it was going to get taken off anyway. A few moments later, he slips his hand under my tee, and fingertips trail up my abdomen and find a breast. He traces the curve to above the nipple, caresses the skin there in small circles. A long sigh escapes my lips.

His hand that's kneading my shoulder pushes a lock of hair behind my ear then rubs the back of my neck, ever so slowly moving upward until he's massaging the back of my head while he caresses my breast. My hips thrust up and back, and I seem to float away to some place that very well may be Heaven.

On the screen, Venus reaches for the masseur's erect cock, rubs it through his boxers, but I'm far more interested in Jeremiah's fingers as they move to the bottom of my tee and pull it up. I raise my arms and let him take it off. I turn to him, unbutton his shirt, then my fingers graze his bare, chiseled chest. I reach for his jeans, unsnap them. He slips them off, as I palm his erection through his boxers. Standing, he slips them off as well, and his full cock, thick and statuesque, rises magnificently before me. Leaning over, he unbuttons my shorts, tugs them off.

I'm not wearing any panties either.

***

Jeremiah looks down at my bald pussy. "I see you remembered."

"I wouldn't want to get any hair between your teeth."

"That's much appreciated." He turns off the movie with the remote then takes his erection in hand and strikes it against my vagina's opening. Sliding his cock up my cleft, he strikes my clit a couple of times with it.

I moan, as my eyes close and back arches.

He grins. "I see you like my lolly hammer."

I chuckle. "Isn't a lolly a lollipop?"

"Yes, and you're welcome to suck on it if you like."

"That wasn't part of the payment arrangement."

"My oversight. Kudos to you on being an excellent negotiator."

"I refuse to ever surrender my power and will assert it whenever I can."

He strikes my clit a couple of more times with his erection, and my hips gyrate toward him, as I let out a little gasp.

"We'll see about that. Get on all fours on the sofa, your ass facing me."

I do, even though the couch is a little small for me. Once I am in position, he gets on his knees behind me, my ass and pussy fully exposed to his face. His large hands hold my thighs so I won't fall off. A moment later, I feel his hot breath on my cleft, and then his tongue makes a long lap across it and my clit.

"Oooooh," I say, and my eyes involuntarily close once more. My hand reaches back, grabs his as it holds my thigh.

His long laps suddenly turn into quick flicks. My neck arches back, as I moan in rhythm to his tongue lashing. My hips thrust up and down.

And then his tongue slows and circles my clit one way then the other over and over. It's a new sensation, soft and sensual after his roughness. The fingers of my free hand go to my mouth.

He backs off my clit, I thought to get air, but instead his lips bite on and pull my folds – another new sensation, one that sends my heart racing. And then his tongue is back on my clit, flicking it and gradually increasing the pace.

I caress my breasts, as my hips gyrate against his face. This power he exerts over me, it's trancelike. Between moans, I bite my lower lip as my body strains. A feeling of ecstasy simmers in me, trying to burst.

My whole body stiffens then spasms, as I let out a long, loud groan. A warm bliss engulfs me, and suddenly nothing matters anymore.

***

Shit, Jeremiah wasn't kidding, I tell myself as returning to Earth, he could make me cum. Which meant next is…I gulp as he rises to his feet.

He gently places his hand in mine. "Stand up."

I try. Knees weak and head dizzy from the orgasm, I more stumble than stand, and right into Jeremiah's arms. His cock bobs against my tummy, and then he carefully sits on the sofa with me standing to his side.

"Now that you've felt some pleasure, it's time to feel some pain," he says.

His large hand grips my wrist and pulls me over his knees, and I squeak.

Jeremiah lets me settle onto his lap, and when all either one of us can hear is our breathing, he snakes a hand under my throat and lifts my head.

His other hand slaps my ass, not hard at all but not exactly gentle. I flinch, then he kisses the back of my head as his palm caresses my ass.

He slaps my bare butt cheeks again. My eyes close and mouth opens, and I find myself breathing harder.

Jeremiah slaps again and then once more, as kissing my hair, and I moan. How does this man exert violent power over me yet show such affection? How is it that I crave both? Would he ever let me be the one with power and control him?

Then his hand takes off on my ass, quickly slapping each cheek, like he is hammering in a nail that he's finally positioned.

"Oooh," I let out, as my ass cheeks burn from his strikes.

His slaps grow in speed, echoing off every wall, as my ass grows more and more tender. My feet claw at the floor, trying to keep my balance, and I shriek. Anticipation of the burn actually proves more painful than the strike itself.

And then the slapping stops.

"You're going to stand up now," he says.

Jeremiah pulls me back and upright, as my hands brace against his muscular thighs.

"Do you know why I stopped?" he says.

I shake my head as rubbing my sore ass.

"Look at my lap."

I stare down at it. Where my pussy had been is wet and his hair matted.

"Touch yourself between your legs," he says.

I bring a hand to my pussy. I am wetter now than when he'd licked me to orgasm. My face reddens.

"Looks like you found some pleasure in the pain." He chuckles. "So, one last installment, and you will be paid up. What is your favorite position?"

I am determined to exert my power over him and to cum one more time. "Cowgirl."

Jeremiah grins. "Of course." He rises, his erection bobbing before him, and steps to a large open spot on the living room floor. He lays down, and with his cock sticking straight up, waves me over. "Climb on, honey."

***

I straddle his lap, my feet tucked into his hips, and lower myself, gasping in pleasure as my pussy fully engulfs his cock. A palm goes to his chest to steady myself as my hips grind against him.

"Your cock is mine," I say. "It's my toy to play with, and I'm going to use it to pleasure myself."

My head tilts back and eyes close. Using my thighs, I lift and lower myself onto his cock, his hips start to respond, and his groans increase in volume each time I drop myself on him.

"My pussy," I get out between gasps. "What...did it...taste like?"

"Like a salted lemon lollipop."

My mouth widens as I try to bring in more air. He moans in pleasure, as I work his cock with my pussy, twisting this way and that on it. A sheen of sweat covers our bodies, and my disheveled hair sticks to my wet face.

Then my arms go behind me, and I plant my palms on his thighs to give myself more leverage. Increasing my speed, my eyes roll to the back of my head. His groans and grunts egg me on.

I bring my hands behind my head, gyrate my hips on his cock, my pussy circling it. Then I lean forward, my hardened nipples right in his face, droplets of sweat falling off my breasts onto his cheeks. I bite my lower lip then smile at him as I grind.

"I'm powerful too," I whisper to him.

"You are. That's what I love about you."

My eyes close. I'm getting close, and my grinds turn to thrusts, as I ride his pole up and down. I sit up, and my palm goes to his chest, the nails digging into his skin.

Our thrusts grow urgent against one another, and then as we both stiffen, his hands grip my hips tight and my nails break his skin. His warm cum spurts deep inside me, and my pussy clenches his cock, as we both groan.

***

We rest naked in one another's arms on the living room carpet, Jeremiah caressing my hair. Being like this feels so right.

Then he gently pushes me away and rises, the light from the hole in the roof shining upon him. I sit up, suddenly feel so alone.

Jeremiah's chiseled chest glistens with our sweat, as he gathers his clothes. "I'll be back tomorrow to finish the roof." He pulls on his boxers.

I gaze at him for a long moment. "Will I ever see you

again after that?"

He tugs up his jeans and winks. "If you want to. I do all kinds of handyman work – landscaping, carpentry, drywalling..."

I watch him finish dressing in silence, and then he leans toward me, and our lips meet, as equals, neither of us trying to take charge or control the other. His cedarwood scent lingers as he pulls back.

A moment later, he's out the door. His truck starts up, then the hum of its engine slowly disappears as he drives away.

Sighing and thinking of that last kiss, I stare at the far wall. I contemplate smashing a hole in it.

Venus Fly Trap

You're a child, I think as looking at his online dating profile, but of course he wasn't. Not anymore. Though I'd seen him playing in a sandbox at the park, tossing a football in the yard with his friends, and backing his parents' car out of the garage for the first time, Grant no longer was a boy. But what the hell was he doing on a site for old women?

Well, not that old. Forty-something...and as horny as they say women in the forties get. I do a quick calculation. He is 21 maybe 22.

And the years have been good to him – well-muscled, hazel eyes that sparkle, a shy smile on his lips, dirty blond hair that's short and wavy. Too bad more men on this site don't take care of themselves like Grant. Too bad more men on this site don't make the first move. For a moment I wonder if Grant might understand my–

A ringing phone jars me from staring at Grant's picture. I glance to see who is calling and instantly blush. *Rebecka.* My best friend. My next door neighbor. Grant's mother.

"Hello?" I answer cautiously. She couldn't know that I was reading her son's dating profile online, could she?

"Adriana, what are you doing?"

I check my window. "Um..." *Seriously contemplating*

writing your son to see if he'd go on a date with me.
"...surfing the Internet."

"Checking out that dating site, I bet!"

I glance out my window again, half expecting to see her staring at me through binoculars. "Um, no..."

"C'mon Adriana, how long have you been divorced from Cecil? Two years? It's time to quit moping around and get out there!"

Three years actually. And in all that time, I haven't been out once, not unless you call an evening with my Lelo smart wand a date. "I know, you're right."

"You bet I am. And that's why I'm calling – unless you're meeting some guy tonight, why don't you go bowling with me and the girls? It's a fundraiser for the local food bank."

Hmm...it does sound fun and is a good cause. At the very least, I won't be tempted to write Grant. "Okay, what time?"

***

Twenty years before...

I'm on bed on all fours, Cecil behind me on his knees, his cock fully nestled in my wet pussy. My hands grip the sheets, and I'm gasping with each thrust, eyes closed. We've only been dating for three months, but I can't keep him waiting any longer...besides, *I* don't want to wait.

He places a palm where my ass meets my lower back. My breathing deepens, my gasps grow louder; this only excites him, and he pumps faster. I bite my lower lip then my mouth widens trying to bring in air. I want to collapse to the bed, I want him to raise that hand and...

Enjoy the moment, I tell myself. He's good in bed, though I should expect that from someone who's five years older than me; by this time in his life, he should know what a woman wants. And he does, oh does he ever.

Except I'm not just any woman.

And then, just as my mouth bites the sheets, as I imagine it's his skin I'm sinking my teeth into, there's a *smack!*

"Ohhh!" I moan into the sheets, as the sting from his palm across my butt cheek spreads.

Oh God, slap me again, I want to say.

And then, before I can work up the courage to speak those words, his hands grip me tight; he makes one last mighty thrust and groans loudly, as his cum fills me.

***

I tie my stinky bowling shoes as the other gals make small talk. How work is going. The need for some sunny days lest the crocuses rot. New recipe adventures. Upcoming anniversary.

"Where's he taking you?" Rebecka asks Dina.

"Jerico's. It's where we first met."

A round of *ahh's* goes up. "Fancy place," Rebecka says.

"Wait – did you say *met*?" Nadia turns to Dina. "So that technically wasn't your first date?"

"No, Kelby was actually there with some other girl, and I was there with some other guy. We kept looking at each other from across the room. When we were about to leave and our dates went to the bathroom, Kelby introduced himself, asked for my number, and well, the rest is history."

Another round of *ahh's* goes up.

Each in turns tells her tale. For Nadia, met at a friend's birthday part. Waiting room at dentist for Rebekah. Online chat room about movies for Aisha. When my turn comes, they all look at me, but I don't answer, and they glance away and fidget.

"All righty, who's ready to knock down some pins?" Rebecka says, as she rises and grabs a bowling ball.

I want to say, *Cecil and I met when we were young; he was just a bit older than Grant. A real gentleman, at least then, he saved a dog that got away from its owner and was running across the street with a car coming straight at it. He ran into the street, grabbed its leash, and yanked it back just in time. Back then, if you liked a guy, you jumped into bed with him if you felt like it, and after seeing that, I felt like it. Even better, I loved the sex. After a long session of foreplay that left my pussy lips swollen and pouting, he'd go down on me. Once I'd cum, I was game for anything he wanted, and when it came to sex positions, he wanted to try them all. Sometimes, when he entered me from behind or if I rode him cowgirl, he'd swat my ass, which sent my clit a-twitchin all over again.*

Gazing off into space, I catch a greasy-haired guy with a little slump checking me out from the next lane. When our eyes lock, he smiles. There's a black gap between his teeth.

Oh where have all the good men gone?

"Your turn, Adriana," Nadia says.

"Oh sorry." I grab a ball and approach the lane, and as my arm swings forward, I remind myself not to cross the line. I knock over nine pins, set myself up for an easy spare.

Halfway through the game, the conversation turns to what our kids are doing. For some reason, no one remembers that Cecil and I never got around to that part of marriage, so Nadia blithely talks about her Brianna loving the university in Kearney, and Aisha tells of her Cristina getting a job in retail at Westroads.

"Grant is at UNO this year?" Dina says.

"Majoring in aviation," Rebecka says proudly.

Another round of *ahh's*.

"He sure is a handsome boy," Nadia says. "I bet the college girls over there are all crazy about him."

I find myself listening a little too closely to Rebecka's answer.

"He's had a few dates," she says, "but he hasn't told me about anybody special. He's living off campus, always coming and going, so I can't easily keep tabs on him."

"Probably for the best," Aisha says. "Sometimes you don't want to know what your children are getting into."

***

Eighteen years before...

I wring my hands as Cecil sits across from me at the restaurant overlooking the Missouri River. Lights sparkle along the riverwalk and the distant interstate bridge. I figure if I tell him in a public place, he's more likely to manage his emotional response should it be one of anger or disgust. It'll still hurt, but if I can curb his reaction, then maybe I can lessen the pain.

"Is everything all right?" Cecil says. "You seem a little...nervous."

Nervous is an understatement. But we've dated for more than a year and have been talking about marriage. I need to tell him before we tie our fortunes together.

For a moment, I wish I had told my previous boyfriends about me, if only so I had some template for use in this conversation.

I take a deep breath. "I have to tell you something about me."

Cecil leans forward, his eyebrows furrowing in concern.

"You're going to think I'm a weirdo."

He merely stares at me, his eyes narrowing.

"I have a kink. I'm a spankophile. I derive sexual pleasure from being spanked."

Cecil leans back, his mouth slightly open on one side, as if processing what I just told him.

"I enjoy our sex. You're a fantastic lover. But it's not entirely satisfying because...because I want to be spanked. I've never faked any orgasm I've had with you, but almost every time I've cum, I've fantasized that you were spanking me."

Still nothing from him.

"I want you to know this before we go any further with..." I choke on this, almost ready to cry. "...our relationship."

His forehead wrinkles, then lips slowly part, as if he's

uncertain what to say. "Well, that's okay. I can deal with that. It's all right."

A sense of liberty washes through me, as if I've just been released from shackles. I rise from my chair, in two strides am before him, then fall into his arms and hug him tight as I cry with joy.

***

Once home from bowling, curiosity gets the better of me. I go online to check out Grant's profile, just to see what he wrote about himself.

A little red *1* shows on my mailbox in the website's upper right corner. Maybe there is hope for me yet. I click on the mailbox, moving the mouse a little faster than usual.

My mouth drops open.

It is from Grant.

Do I open it? If I do, he'll get a message saying I did. Well, if it gets awkward, I always can feign ignorance.

So I click the message. It reads:

Surprised to see you on here! How's it panning out?

Hmm, that's safe enough. Not responding makes me look embarrassed and unneighborly, though. Responding would be harmless if I can figure out what to say.

I type:

Surprised to see you too. Not much luck. I'd like us to remain platonic.

Remain platonic? No, that would just tell him I'm not interested. Wait, what am I thinking? Of course I'm not interested!

I delete that.

Well, maybe I should start flirting, just for the fun of it. I am out of practice. I type:

Surprised to see you too. I'm glad you wrote. Thinking of you makes me smile.

No, that would send the wrong message. You're not interested, Adriana, remember?

I type:

Surprised to see you too. Not much luck. I'm having a difficult time meeting guys on this site. So many of them seem to be here just for sex or to find a woman who'll be their maid. And when I do find someone interesting, I'm not quite sure what to say to them. I feel so intimidated and old.

No, no, no, that's too heavy. It'll turn him off. Okay, I *am* interested.

I delete my response and close my laptop. There's no need to do anything until I figure out what to say.

Heading into my bedroom, I undress and pull my ever faithful smart wand from the nightstand drawer. I can't seem to get Grant's beautiful hazel eyes out of my head. I lay tummy down on the bed, turn on the wand, and place it between my legs so the vibrating head touches my pussy. A wave of loneliness washes over me, as my finger reaches to my butt and gives me a rim job. I let out a soft moan.

***

Seventeen years before...

We marry, we buy our first place together, we experiment with spanking during sex.

Sometimes we do it in a playful context, like joking around or losing a bet. Nice, but like an overly sweet cookie it doesn't satisfy my hunger.

Sometimes we do it simply because he knows that's what I want. Good, but like small talk with a neighbor, it doesn't satisfy my need for intimacy.

Then one time he sends me to the corner to stand for 10 minutes before my promised spanking. I grow wetter with each passing minute, wondering what's next.

When my corner time is up, he grabs my wrist, drags me toward the bed, and once he sits on the edge, yanks me over his lap. My bottom trembles, as my slit throbs.

"This is for your own good," he says.

Smack!

His palm comes down full force on my ass cheeks, and I let out a yip of surprise. His hand doesn't stop, going from cheek to cheek, as a fire breaks out on my bottom.

Soon I'm howling like a scalded cat, rubbing my clit against his thigh, as his palm smacks my ass over and over, and then comes a white, hot flash of pleasure spreading through my body.

Yes, I think to myself, *that's how I want it be, forever and ever.*

***

I rise early for work and open the blinds to check the weather. Across the yard in Rebecka's house, a silhouette of she and her husband kissing stands out against her light curtains. I stare for a moment then walk away.

Coffee. That's what I do next each morning, make coffee.

As the coffee brews, I log onto the dating app. Maybe last night some guy who will sweep me away with passion and deep desire joined. I page through profiles. One guy says he's not short, just "fun sized." Hmm, 5'3" is short. Another guy says he's healthy and fit. The gut hanging over his belt buckle begs to differ. One guy has three kids from three different women. Not *wives*?

The app's DM screen pops up.

Good morning, Adriana.

It's Grant.

And we're now apparently on a first-name basis with one another. Well, I should hope so after last night, tee-hee.

I also realize there's no more ignoring him, not unless that's the message I want to send. Somehow I feel like a butterfly pulled into a Venus fly trap.

Before I can type anything, he adds:

I was just listening to Avril Lavigne and thinking of you.

Because she's from two decades ago or because she has something new out that reminds you of me? Well, at least he gives me a safe, platonic entry into a conversation. I type:

Yeah? You like her music?

Three dots flash a couple of times then comes his response:

Yeah. Complicated and My Happy Ending are great

songs.

OK, so he's got great taste in music. Which is the same thing my mother would have said if one of my classmates told her he liked Air Supply. I type:

How are your studies going?

OK, lame, I know.

Great, he responds. *Love my classes. Should get a good internship this summer, hoping they'll later hire me. They pay really well.*

Which is better than most of the guys on this dating app can say for their careers. I type:

You're not coming back to your mother's this summer?

More blinking dots then:

Probably not but don't tell her.

Oh trust me, I'll *never* tell her.

Then before I can type a response, he writes:

Hey, wanna get together for coffee some time? Catch up with one another?

Well, there it is, the game show host has asked me which door I want to open. I do want to meet, but he is asking me to do so on an online dating app. Yet our conversation has been platonic; there's no reason to think our meeting wouldn't be as well. What to do, what to do? The clock is ticking. I write:

That would be great.

He quickly responds:

Awesome! How 'bout Cuppa Oasis? Saturday morn at 10?

I pause. He seems a little enthusiastic about meeting. Well, how do I back out now without fibbing? Besides, I actually do want to meet. Just to get out of the house for a while, I lie to myself. I write:

Okay. See you then.

I quickly log off before he can write anything more.

***

Sixteen years before...

While at work, my cell phone chimes with a new text. Cecil writes:

Report to me at 6 p.m. sharp, young lady. You've been a naughty girl, and you need a good, sound spanking.

Butterflies of excitement buzz in my belly when I read the word *spanking.* I can't wait to go home. I glance at the clock on my computer. 10:30 a.m.

Cecil gets it at last. It's not about the pain. It's about the verbiage, the anticipation, the sexiness of letting go.

For the next few hours, I squirm uncomfortably in my chair.

***

I sit next to the tall windows, watching the rain fall that Saturday in April, drinking a latte, waiting. There's something about being older that makes you think you need to be there a few minutes before the appointed time, but somehow I'd forgotten that the young are not bound by the clock; to them, time seems to stretch out to infinity. At last I spot Grant coming up the sidewalk, and when he enters Cuppa Oasis, I wave at him.

His hazel eyes stay on me, as his powerful arms swing back and forth in rhythm with a confident walk. He wears a tight black T-shirt, and his muscles ripple as he moves. He looks better in person than in his pictures.

After ordering a coffee, Grant slides into the chair across from me at my bistro table. He smells of cream and the woods. "Thanks for meeting, Adriana," he says with his alluring smile.

"Hello Grant. Sounds like you're having a great year at college."

"I am. Good grades, expanding my horizons, and discovering much about myself."

Hmm, *discovering*. I decide not to ask just quite yet what he's learning about himself.

"Looks like you've been working out."

His smile broadens. "Thanks for noticing. You must be hitting the gym yourself."

My cheeks blush, and I suppress a laugh. "Me in a gym? Maybe long ago when I was in school, but I haven't been to one in a while."

"You couldn't tell."

Damn, I think he's flirting with me.

Damn, I think I like it.

Damn, damn, damn.

"Grant..." I look at my coffee, trace the rim of it with my finger, the look up at him. "...what are you doing on a dating site for older women?"

I expect him to turn red at that, but his happy expression doesn't change at all. "You know how I said this past year has been one of discovery for me?"

"Mhm-mhm."

"Well, I've been attracted to women older than me for some time. As a child, I always thought they were prettier than my teenage babysitters, and in high school,

I often caught myself staring at them. This past year, since I was away from home, I decided it was time to explore further, and soon found himself trawling the Internet for...adventure."

I nod slowly. So that's why he hardly ever dated anyone in high school. "Have you found an alluring woman who's got you under her seductive spell?"

"Maybe. I'm not sure yet. The thing is, I don't want a cougar who treats me like her little cub. I want a woman who will let me take the lead."

Given a young man's inexperience, a cougar usually wants to be in charge. "Do you think an older woman would do that?"

"I think some would. You see, it's a generational thing. So many young women today want everything in a relationship to be equal. It's...well, emasculating. Many older woman are still from that era when they had no problem with a man...taking charge."

Oh, how very old school. Stereotypes everywhere. Still, I am guilty of them myself, I think. Older men – well, way older compared to Grant – tend to make sure you were pleased, but after you each came, it was all over if only because they were exhausted. I imagine younger men are able to keep pounding you all night until you say *no more*. My heart thuds.

Grant leans in. "Not that I mean to change the subject, but I've always admired how nice your house looked, you know how it was decorated and everything matched."

"Oh. Thank you."

"Maybe I could get your opinion on what color my curtains should be, given my furniture?"

"What color is your sofa?"

"It's sort of an off blue, darker than sky blue but lighter than regular blue. It's kind of hard to explain. Which is why I'm having trouble finding something to match. Maybe you could come over and look at it. I actually live just a few blocks away."

I suppress a giggle. Give him credit for trying to be subtle. I gaze at him, at how his hazel eyes catch glints of light, find myself having that same feeling I had so long ago. Well, I suppose it wouldn't hurt… "Sure," I say. "I'd be happy to take a look."

"Wanna go now?"

My latte *is* getting cold. "Okay."

***

Six years before…

I hold the packet of birth control pills over the toilet, ready to pop them out and let each one swirl away. This is the only way I can ensure he doesn't think I've deceived him.

But I can't bring myself to do it.

People are starting to look at us; I know they're talking about us behind our backs. He doesn't want children, wants to focus on other things – travel, our careers – says that we owe it to the world to not further burden it with another human being it can't support.

In the quiet of the night, I ponder why I've agreed with him for so long. We've already gone everywhere I've wanted to go. It's his career, not mine, that has taken off. *We* can support a child just fine; Cecil's five years on me means he makes plenty of money that a young couple never could hope to earn, and for that I'm grateful.

I don't care what the others say, not really. In truth, I want something to fill – to bridge – the empty gulf growing between us.

He understands my spanking kink – why can't he understand this?

Popping that pill from the blister pack, watching it fall into the toilet bowl, letting nature take its course, it would be so easy...

My hand brings the packet back to the medicine cabinet. I quick push one out and toss it into my mouth, swallow. I love him too much to be dishonest.

Somehow I'll get him to understand...

***

Grant's place is decorated in that recognizable college pad style. A pennant for UNO's team. A poster of some currently popular singer. A carpet that needs vacuuming. A slightly tattered sofa I remember being in much better shape when it sat in his parents' living room years ago.

"I'm glad we're able to catch up," he says. "Would you like something to drink? I have wine."

Grant brings me a cheap white, and we spend the afternoon chatting. Where I'd traveled and where he'd like to go. What I do for a job and what he intends to do for one. Goals we have in life. What we imagine our dream partner to be like. He makes no moves, gives no indication that this is anything but platonic. A deep relief of feeling accepted, understood and connected overcomes me. I believe I can tell him anything. Well, almost anything.

The darkening walls suggest evening is approaching.

"Would you like to stay for dinner?" he says. "I make a great spaghetti."

It must be the drink or maybe it is the attention because I accept his invite.

As he heads to the kitchen, and I follow, the sobs of a crying child breaks through his apartment. We go to the window, see a little girl in tears next to a tree. No one seems to be watching her.

"Let's see if she needs help," Grant says.

Once outside, I walk up to the little girl and kneel. "Hey honey, what's wrong?"

The little girl points to a branch up in my tree. "Bella won't come down."

We look up at a little kitten hugging the branch, its eyes wide with fright.

"I can get it," Grant says. Near the tree's trunk, he jumps up and grabs hold of the branch's thickest section then pulls himself onto it. It sways a little from his weight, and the kitten's eyes grow even larger, as it meows for help. He shimmies a little farther out onto the branch until he can reach out and grab the kitten. Once he does, he brings it to his chest then jumps to the ground and hands Bella back to the little girl, who is all smiles.

She nuzzles the kitten against her cheek and closes

her eyes. "You've been a very naughty kitten. You scared me!"

Grant and I smile at one another. He steps toward me and suddenly his legs are up in the air, and his back splashes into a mud puddle.

He sits up in it, face red but still grinning. There's mud all over him.

My jaw drops. "Are you all right?"

"Yeah," he laughs. "Guess I should be careful where I step."

He's so embarrassed, it's endearing actually. And that scares me. "I should be going," I tell him.

"No, no," he quick says, as rising. "I just need to quick shower then I'll make dinner." He holds out his arm for me to help him up.

I take his muddy hand. It feels so warm, so comforting. A moment later, he's back on his feet.

"Well, spaghetti *does* sound good."

***

Three years ago...

The last time we have sex, he slowly slides down my lacy panties, keeping his hands flush to my skin all the way to my ankles. I watch in anticipation, and my breathing hitches. He flicks the thin material to the side and places both hands behind my knees. My chest rises and falls with exhilaration, as he lifts both legs over his shoulders, bringing my ass off the mattress, though I'm not sure how he'll spank me in this position.

Before I know it, his cock is at my slit. I close my eyes and ride the pleasure, as he pounds into me. The headboard slams against the wall. I crave the feel of his hard body, want to run my hands over his chest and shoulders, want his palm to smack my ass, which meets only air. It's like he wants to punish me. But I let him have control, let him fuck me as he sees fit.

I'll get my turn, I tell myself.

Then his head tosses back, and he groans with pleasure. His warm cum fills me. Once he catches his breath, he lets go of my legs, curls up next to me.

The last time we have sex, he doesn't spank me.

***

The shower's spray roars to life, splashing against the bathtub and wall tiles. I notice he's left the bathroom door open, and I creep toward it, peak around the doorjamb.

Grant's silhouette through the light shower curtain shows off all of his muscles. A flush creeps across my chest.

How long has passed since I've seen a man naked? Since I've been touched by that man? For a moment, I contemplate joining him.

What would he say if he saw me naked with my breasts starting to sag and cellulite starting to gather on my thighs? Wouldn't he be turned off? Did he really like older women?

Then Grant's shout booms over the shower's thunderous spray. "Hey Adriana!"

I wait a couple of beats to respond, so he doesn't realize I'm just outside the door. "Yes?"

"I forgot my towel – could you get one out of the

dryer for me? It's next to the bedroom."

I look down the hall and spot a stacked washer-dryer combo in a recess. Sure enough, there's a bunch of towels in the dryer.

I bring one to the bathroom, take a tentative step inside. Grant's toned arms are bent up as fingers rub shampoo through his hair, all of it a monochrome gray through the curtain. My hand runs up my stomach and between the breasts. I set the towel on the toilet seat next to the bathtub. Her turns slightly, reaches for soap, and I see his curved cock, hanging before him. I should leave, but...

"Grant, can you keep a secret?" I say.

He scrubs his broad shoulders with soap. "Sure."

"It's been three years since I've had sex."

He stops scrubbing.

"It's been three years since a man has touched me."

He's still standing there, but his cock suddenly is semi-hard.

"Your mother can never find out."

Grant stops, turns toward me, only the flimsy, barely translucent shower curtain between us. He partially open it. "There's room for one more in here."

I undress slowly, letting him enjoy the show, as he watches me through the curtain. Then I pull it partially aside and step in, see him fully naked for the first time.

"Let me get you cleaned up," Grant says, and we maneuver past one another – my breasts brush against his chest, and his hard cock against my thighs – to switch places.

The spray of water droplets, like warm rain from the shower head, hits my back, filling the bathtub with a foggy haze that penetrates the tightness in my shoulders, as we gaze into one another's eyes. I dip my head down; the beads of water saturate my hair before trickling down my back and face then down onto my feet below.

His hands hold my upper arms, as if bracing me. His touch feels better than the warm water.

Grant's head moves closer to me, and I toward him, and his lips, soft and supple, graze mine. He pulls back. "You're very beautiful, Adriana."

He reaches for the soap, rubs it between his hands, then lathers all my body – the neck, the shoulders, my hips and tummy, my breasts, which releases a low moan from me, then down my thighs and legs. Turning me around he takes care of my back and ass, spending extra time on the latter. As he rinses me off, my soapy hand runs up and down his dick.

***

Two years before...

It's a double death.

When Cecil and I break up, I lose not just a loved one but the security that comes with someone who knows your spanking fetish. That you are a spanko is not something you can just announce to the world.

Before him, I was always watching, waiting, for even the smallest sign that a man might be accepting of me. Now I'm back to that, to crouching in the darkness hoping I am not preyed upon.

As a child, I always was interested in and curious about others who were spanked by their parents. I suddenly find myself wondering if other women who walk around happy have found a man who spanks then afterward cares for them.

Before meeting Cecil, I'd trawl dating site after dating site, looking for someone who might leave some hidden message in their profile, some wording that lets me know they are willing to be a loving spankee. I am surprised to find some of my accounts from before Cecil still exist and can be reactivated.

***

We step out of the shower, drying off one another, giving extra attention to our private parts. I feel young again, young and dirty. Very dirty.

"You've been a very naughty kitten," he says and slaps my butt.

Oh, that is a good sign.

"Perhaps you could recommend a curtain color to match my bedspread?" he says.

I follow him naked into his bedroom, stand at the side of the bed, which surprisingly is a queen. The bedspread is navy blue, a typical male choice. As thinking of what would match, my finger caresses the bedspread. It's smooth and clean.

Grant's hands grip my upper arms again, and he turns me around, kisses me. His lips graze mine, as a whisper might an ear, then they are firm and powerful. I inhale his scent of cream and the woods. Pulling back, we gaze into one another's eyes, then he pushes me back onto the bed. I let out a yelp and find myself laying on it with my legs over the side. He drops to his knees between my legs and pushes the thighs apart.

He slowly licks my labia then along the wet slit. My eyes close. His tongue slips in, circling my entrance then across my clit. I let go a low moan, as the warmth of his mouth covers my pussy.

Then he pulls back. I lift my head to see what he's about to do, to tell him to keep licking rather than to start fucking me. He has no intention of the latter, though. His hands come together, as if to pray, then his middle finger slips into my pussy. Another finger spreads my labia, and I feel his hot breath on my swollen clit. His thumbs support his chin, as his tongue finds my clit.

My eyes roll to the back of my head as my neck arches. Hmm, which older woman taught him this?

His tongue circles around my clit, barely touching it, like the fluttering of soft flower petals against a cheek. He maintains a slow, steady pace, sometimes going clockwise, sometimes counterclockwise. As he does, his wet tongue presses evermore on my clit, as if the petals were closing on it, trapping it. My hips grind against him, as every muscle tightens in anticipation.

Then the tension across my body releases, and I pulse in pleasure, as letting out a long moan of satisfaction.

That sure beat my smart wand.

***

One year before...

I spend a long time on his profile, wanting to reply.

His pictures show him smiling as he walks through the woods with his dog, as he holds his toddler nephew at a birthday party. He's got a nice smile, a slim but fit build, dark hair.

What's wrong with him, I wonder.

He likes hiking, eating out, traveling. Tick, tick, tick each box of my interests. But there's one he doesn't mention.

There must be something wrong with him. He should have a girlfriend.

He explains what he's looking for in a partner – someone to share his time with, someone he can talk to, someone who's smart and likes to laugh. He's open to having children.

One photo shows some tiny pits and pockmarks along part of his jawline. Maybe that's why no one is with him. Hmm, nothing that a sexy beard wouldn't cover.

Good paying job, tick. In middle management no less. College education, tick. No complaining or crude language. Tick.

My cursor hovers over the Like button. *No, do one better, write to him.* I move the cursor to the Contact button.

No, don't. I already can tell the first coffee date will go well. We'll fall in love. And then, as we inch toward engagement, I'll have to tell him. He'll think I'm a weirdo.

I close the window for the dating app, and my head bows in defeat.

***

Grant rises, his hard dick bobbing.

I sit up hold out my hand to stop. "Not yet. Sit on the edge of the bed."

He takes a seat in the spot I patted.

"Did you enjoy licking my pussy?"

He nods. "It tasted like salted honey. Delicious." His hazel eyes are dark, soldering.

I stand, and he suddenly looks surprised, as if his luck has run out. *Au contraire, Grant.*

Before he can speak, I shimmy over his lap so his hard cock touches my tummy. "I need to atone for crossing the line. Will you spank me...*please*?"

I don't have to ask twice. He holds one of my hips with his hand, pushing my body against him, and with the free hand slaps a butt cheek. Then he slaps the other.

"Hmmm," I murmur and feel his cock twitch.

He massages my ass cheeks then squeezes them. Then he goes back to slapping them, and I moan with each strike. My pussy tingles.

His hand slips between my legs, and feeling my wetness, rubs my clit for several seconds. My hips gyrate against his leg, and with that he begins slapping my ass again.

"Harder," I say.

He pauses a moment, as if contemplating my request. Then he follows through.

I flinch. "Ahh," I murmur, and my hands clench his legs.

His hard palm strikes again, and this time the sting lingers. Then again and again until the burn won't go away. My wet pussy lips suction his thigh.

I lower my hips downwards, as if to avoid Grant's heavy, even slaps and have a momentary shock of pleasure as realizing how good grinding my clit into the edge of his thigh feels.

"*Faster,*" I say.

He massages my ass cheeks, then squeezes them, shaping and molding them as if they were Play-Doh.

And then his assault begins afresh. He slaps one ass cheek hard three times in as many seconds then the same with the other ass cheek, then repeats again, as I yelp and hump his leg until my clit rubs against his bare skin and I cum.

Before I can fully catch my breath, his muscular arms raise me off him and toss me onto the edge of the bed. "Get on all fours," he says.

I do, and my legs below my knees hang over the bed's edge. He pushes my thighs apart again and penetrates me.

"Ohhhh," I gasp. My breathing quickens and hips move in rhythm to his steady thrusts.

His large hands grip my waist, and the sound of his thighs slapping my ass fills the room as he jackhammers me. I pull his pillow beneath my head, grip it tight. Biting my lower lip, I gasp as he grunts with each thrust.

Grant's hand reaches forward, pulls my hair. My eyes close, as he draws my head off the pillow. "Oh yes," I moan.

His hand slides down to my neck, grips the back of it as releasing my hair. He wants me. At this moment, he wants me like no other man does.

How he's able to keep going, I wonder. Not that I want him to stop.

His other hand comes around to my throat, and he brings a finger to the lips; I suck it into my mouth, as he fucks me. I'm getting close.

"Yes, yes, yes, oh yes," he groans, then gives one last great thrust and a loud, guttural moan, as his warm cum sprays into me.

He holds me in place, while his cock fills me with what little is left in him, and fleeting thoughts of being spanked trip through my head. An instant later, every one of my muscles tenses then releases, and I descend into a velvet black, calm and peaceful, no pain anywhere in my body or the universe.

***

We crawl to the head of the bed, curl up in one another's naked bodies.

"After you spank me, it's very important that we cuddle for a long time," I tell him as nestling me head into his chest. "I need the...comforting."

He nods. Once his breathing finally slows, he whispers, "Thank you."

I half giggle. "You don't need to thank me."

"No, I must, Adriana. I've always found it difficult to explain to women older than me why I was so attracted to them, why I only felt sexually aroused by them and not by girls my age. I always felt like something was wrong with me, that–"

I bring a finger to his lips. "Shh. You don't need to explain. I understand."

The tenseness in his face left. "You do?"

"It's no big deal. It's all right."

My hand reaches down to his semi-hard cock. In a couple of strokes, he's fully erect again. "Lay back," I tell him, and once he does, I climb atop then position his cock at my pussy entrance. In one quick drop, I sheathe it, and we both moan in pleasure.

I run a finger along his lips. "My *man* never needs to explain anything to me."

Humiliations Chéries

Étrange, n'est-ce pas? I whispered aloud as Jason walked toward me, his steps slow and determined, his chest held high. *Does he think I'll just jump into bed with him too?*

He stopped at my beach blanket, close enough that I could count all six of his abs. "I hope you don't mind me saying," he said, "but you have an incredible smile."

Was I smiling when he was walking toward me? "I was just thinking of what a nice view I had."

He chuckled. "I'm Jason."

"Yeah, I know who you are," I said as grinning. "You fucked my little sister earlier this summer."

His eyes widened. "I, uh–sorry, I didn't realize. Guess I'll be going–"

"What? I'm not as good looking as my little sis?" I interrupted.

His jaw dropped. "No, um, you're prettier actual–"

"Damn right I am. Sit down, stud."

He hesitantly sat at the edge of the beach blanket. "So, uh, how is Laura? She is your sister right? There's a...family resemblance."

"I don't mean to disappoint you, but Laura was less interested in you than your cock. She's moved on to screwing other guys."

His face paled.

Yeah, like a girl would fall in love with you just for your cock.

"I'm, um...surprised you let me sit here."

"Why's that?

"Well...you must not think all that highly of me and–"

"You're right, I don't," I interrupted again. "Why don't you show me that I'm wrong?"

Ocean blue eyes beneath a mop of shaggy blond hair scanned my expression, and apparently satisfied that I was flirting, his body relaxed. "I vaguely remember you from high school. You were a couple of classes ahead of me, weren't you?"

"Apparently ahead of you in more than just classes." *Good, keep him off balance.*

His brow furrowed. "I'm sorry for being a jerk. I marched over here to hit on you, and I can see now that was disrespectful of me." He started to get up.

"Don't go yet. I like a man who realizes he's fucked up and apologizes for it. That's a rare quality."

His face blushed pink. Maybe he thought I caught him telling a lie. "Are you going to college?" Jason said, as sitting back down.

"UC Santa Barbara, French lang and lit major. Say, when they hell are you going to ask me my name?"

His cheeks reddened. "Um, I'm Jason and–"

"I know *your* name. It's the only name Laura said for two whole days after you two screwed."

He brightened at that. *Time to take him down a notch.*

"And then she jumped into bed with Brandon, and all I heard for the next two days was his name, and then it was Kevin and then Shawn...I think she's up to Randy now."

The spirit in his eyes dwindled. After that retort, I wasn't sure why he stuck with me. I guess men really do think with their cocks rather than their heads.

"Um, your name is Ariel, right?"

My eyebrows rose. "Hmm, very good, Jason. I'm impressed."

He perked a little. "Hey, want a shaved ice?"

Oh my, a man who knows the way to my heart. "Sure."

We rose, then as taking a step toward the concession stand, I grabbed his forearm and said, "You do have money to pay for this, right?"

"Um, yeah. Of course."

"All tight then, stud, I'm all yours until the cup is empty." I hooked my arm inside his, gently brought his forearm up so we were walking arm in arm. The firmness of his muscles felt good, kind of protective, against my thinness.

I surreptitiously glanced at the front of his swimming trunks to see if this was doing something for him. *Maybe. Or maybe he really is just well hung like li'l sis claimed.*

"Laura said you were really smart," he said.

"You like to talk about Laura a lot, don't you?"

"No, I uh–"

"Relax stud, I'm just playing with you. And yeah, I am smart. Is that a problem?"

"Not at all, I like smart girls."

I laughed. "Then what were you doing with my li'l sis?"

"Um, I thought I wasn't supposed to talk about her."

I patted his arm. "Very good. I think you're finally getting smart too."

We reached the concession stand. "What's your favorite shaved ice?" he said.

"Lilikoi."

"Lily-koy?"

"Passion fruit."

"Oh...um..."

Better simplify it for him. "It's an orange color. What's yours?"

"Cherry."

I smirked. "Uh huh." *I bet he likes vanilla ice cream too. Well, he did fuck Laura.*

After he paid, we walked, a bit directionless at first, so I veered us toward the water. The beach sand warmed my feet, as the Pacific surf languidly struck the shore. Just before reaching the wet sand, I shifted so we paralleled the ocean.

"Want a tip?" I said.

He shrugged as if to say *sure.*

"Say something nice about me."

"Um, Ariel is a pretty name."

I grinned. "Well, I'm glad you think so. Anything else?"

"Well, you have a terrific smile. I could see it from way across the beach."

Hmm, repetitive, but I still looked at him and squeezed his arm. "You are indeed getting smarter." I offered him my cup. "Wanna taste?"

"Is it safe?"

I laughed. "No it's not. I should collapse any moment now from it."

He gave me his boyish grin and leaned toward the straw.

"Just don't slobber all over it," I said.

A draught of orange ice shot up the straw into his mouth. "Mhm, that is good." He held his cup toward me. "Wanna taste?"

"I already know what cherry tastes like."

He chuckled. "I like your sense of humor. At first I didn't know what to make of it, but I'm getting it now."

"I'm glad. Most people don't like me because of it."

"Oh. You must feel alone sometimes."

"Hey, are you my psychoanalyst now?"

"Sorry, I didn't mean to–"

"Ha! Gotcha!"

Jason rolled his eyes. "Okay, maybe I don't totally get it."

"The beginning of understanding is acknowledging your lack of understanding."

His blond eyebrows twisted slightly, as if he were puzzling over what I'd said.

We'd reached the end of the beach and entered a small, isolated cove. Dunes blocked anyone's view of us. Warm sand shifted between my toes.

"Looks like you want to protect me from all my

would-be suitors, don't you?" I said. "That's very chivalrous of you."

He grinned. "You shouldn't trust those other guys."

I took a seat in the sand and patted the spot next to me. "Let's watch the surf a while."

He sat, and for a few minutes we remained quiet and stared at the ocean, a slight breeze off the waters making for a temperate July day.

"You know, I'm not like my sister," I said at last.

His eyebrows fell as he frowned.

"Don't look so sad. All that really means is I'm not going to throw myself at you."

His eyes widened, as his mouth let out a barely audible but long "Ohhh," then his forehead wrinkled. Yeah, Jason finally knew he could have me, but he'd have to work for it. He probably wondered, too, if he was up to the task.

I decided to help him along. Leaning toward him, I brushed back a shock of his blond hair. Those ocean blue eyes gazed back at me. "You were right about me being lonely," I said.

His lips brushed over mine, soft and gentle, hesitant. And then I intensified things, grabbing the back of his head and kissing him hard, and when our mouths opened, I gripped his jaw and pulled his tongue deep into my mouth. The whole beach swirled around us.

When we pulled back from one another, he was breathing deeply with this look of *Wow* on his face. *Yeah, li'l sis never kissed you like that.*

My mouth remained flat, though, and his brow slowly

furrowed.

He said, "Wasn't it good for you–"

"*Don't* ask me that. Don't *ever* ask a woman that."

I could have sworn he'd actually slid a little away from me. "Oh. Um, why?"

"Because, stud, you look like you lack confidence. And if there's one thing a woman wants, it's a man with confidence. A man who is *viril*, as the French would say."

He mulled that over for a moment. "Oh."

"I bet my li'l sis didn't ever put your confidence to the test, did she? Probably just opened her legs for you, and afterward you thought you were King Phallus of the beach, didn't you?"

"I – I'm sorry. I didn't mean to piss you off–"

"And *stop* apologizing. That also makes you look like you have no confidence. Confidence is a turn-on for women. You want to turn them on, don't you?"

"Well, yeah–"

"Then make the next move, stud."

"Um, okay." He leaned toward me, and with fumbling fingers, unhooked my bikini top's front clasps then slid the straps down my arms. My breasts tumbled out, the sun warming them. "May I–" he started but then stopped and gently ran his fingers across the top then down the sides and under them. I closed my eyes, felt the first tingle between my legs since we'd been together.

And then he backed off, tugged at my bikini bottoms. I raised my butt off the sand, but kept my thighs closed. Once he slipped them over my feet, he stood, his erection a large bulge in his swimming trunks. He pulled the trunks outward – I supposed so they wouldn't catch on his member – and then dragged them down his legs and stepped out of them. His cock rose in front of him, solid and smooth, the purple head almost reaching his belly button, while his balls hung beneath the base. I had to fight to keep my breath from hitching.

"You're not very deft," I said, "but you have other attributes that…make up for it."

He just stood there, though, the ocean breeze ruffling the hair around his balls, as if he wasn't quite sure what to do next.

"I'm taking charge from here, stud," I said. "The good news is despite everything you're probably going to get to stuff that huge cock in me. But I expect you to make me cum first. Get on your knees."

He slowly lowered himself as I leaned back on my elbows and spread my legs.

"You can start by licking my clit. I'll guide you as we go along. Don't get any sand in there."

Jason lay on his tummy, head between my thighs. His hands separated my thighs, fully exposing my heat to him. His tongue worked at the folds of my slit, lathering them then pushing them aside. I let go a low murmur, as the tip of his tongue grazed my clit. That graze probably was by accident, for he focused on the opening of my vagina.

"Up a little, stud, above my hole," I said softly.

He obliged, and my eyes rolled to the back of my head, as I moaned. His tongue first flicked then circled and swabbed my clit, and he repeated that pattern over and over until my hips involuntarily gyrated to his ministrations.

"Are your fingers...clean...of sand?" I somehow got out.

"Mhm-mhm," he said, and the vibrations of his voice against my clit left it tingling even more.

"Put a finger...inside me."

His finger slowly screwed into my vagina, picking up my juices. I wanted to clamp down on it, to hold it there, but had something better in mind.

"Rub it against...the top of my hole."

His finger pressed upward, touching my G-spot. A wave of pleasure broke over me. *Good, he's not only deep enough but in line with it.*

"Bend your...finger toward yourself," I got out while his tongue continued to work my clit.

The pad of his finger ran against the spongy top of my vagina, and something akin to an electric current ran though me.

"Ohhhh," I said. "Right there. Move your finger...back...and forward, like you're using it to tell me to...'come here.'"

Jason did, and my tissue there swelled. Every muscle in my body tensed.

"Keep doing...*that.*"

Then came a rising warmth and tremor between my thighs, and my whole body shook, as I squirted across his finger and his chin.

"*Oh Jésus, putain de Christ!*" I gasped, as my body

calmed, and I pushed Jason's head away from my pussy.

He stood on his knees and wiped his chin with the back of his arm. "What happened?"

"Not bad," I said catching my breath. "Not bad. You made me squirt, stud. You're pretty damn good when you can make a woman do that."

His chin rose slightly as he smiled. His cock looked even larger than when he'd first taken off his shorts.

"But you know what your problem is?" I said.

The confident look on his face dissolved into a puddle of self-doubt. "My problem?"

"It's that you're still not very bold with me."

His brow furrowed. "What do you mean?"

Of course it made no sense to him. He'd just ate out a naked woman on a beach in broad daylight. How was that not bold?

"You see, my little sis made you feel all Alpha because she was easy. But I'm making you work for it. What you don't understand is *I* don't want to work for it. I want you to be assertive. I'm egging you on to be assertive."

He just stood there on his knees staring at me, probably wondering what the hell I was talking about. What did I expect; it's not like my li'l sis was all that bright either.

"Look, I'll make it easy for you." I turned around and got on all fours. "Spank me."

"What?"

"Spank me. Tell me I'm a bad girl."

A moment later, he slapped a butt cheek, like he was brushing away some branch on a walk in the woods.

"Not like that," I said. "Harder."

He slapped again, this time with a little more force. I think I even heard a little echo off the sand dune.

"Harder."

He took the next slap up a notch. Almost there.

"*Harder.*"

Whack!

I let out a gasp in surprise and winced. "Yeah, like that. Again. Over and over."

Jason struck first one cheek then another. My torso jolted forward, as I felt the singe on my butt cheek. Then it was a steadily increasing rhythm, like a bolero, and my fingers dug into the sand, tried to keep me steady as my ass burned. *Enfin!*

Jason's hand went to the small of my back, held me in place; it was all I could do to not kick up my calves as he slapped. "You're a bad girl," he said, "nothing but a cheap slut." My strategy worked – with each whack, the bolder and more turned on he got.

Then my front arms collapsed, and I held myself up by the elbows, as his slaps grew louder than the waves. His hands grabbed onto my ass and pulled the cheeks apart, exposing my already wet pussy. He repositioned himself behind me, then his cockhead parted me.

With a quick thrust, he filled me, and I moaned deeply.

Jason's hands gripped my hips, and I found myself gasping as his thrusts pushed me forward through the sand, but then his strong hands tightened to hold me in place so his cock could drive into me again. My eyes closed, as I savored the pleasure.

Thwack!

He slapped my ass as he fucked me, and I moaned with each strike. I never wanted that large cock of his to leave me. My muscles increasingly tensed, and I felt myself getting close again.

His thrusts grew more rapid, while his hand held me tighter, his fingers pressing into my skin. Then he tensed and roared as his cum shot into me. My body shook again, and I let out a scream as cumming with him. A warm, floaty feeling overcame me, and my mouth grew dry.

For the next several seconds, he slowly slid in and out, forcing the last of his cum into me. At last, he fell back onto the beach.

I turned around, let the sand cool my burning ass, and grinned at him as his cum dripped onto my thigh. "You know, I still don't think much of you, but my sis was right – you do have a great cock and sure know how to use it."

He chuckled, as he gradually caught his breath, his hands on his red knees.

I jumped up and waded into the water, washed myself off. After a moment, he joined me. We splashed around a little, but to a woman like me that's interesting for only so long, so I went back to shore and redonned my bottoms and top. He frowned then followed and pulled on his shorts. His cock still stood as half-mass, as arm in arm we headed back to my blanket. The glow of the orange sun rippled across the blue water.

"Wow, I didn't realize it was this late," I said as kneeling to pack up my belongings. "I better get going."

Jason nervously crossed then uncrossed his arms over his chest, surprising since I just let him spank then fuck me doggy style on the beach. I could tell he was going to be a project.

"Can I, uh, see you again?" he said at last.

I snickered, then with my beach bag full, rose, leaned toward him, and purred into his ear, "I will find you." *Au revoir, stud.*

My palm swatted his cute little butt, and I walked away into the sunset.

Vile and Foul

"I've done vile things...foul things."

"She did! Give her a good spanking," Kasie shouts, as she raises her glass of wine at the TV.

"Yeah, take her right over your knee," I add, and we laugh. Porn can be so stupid even when it's supposedly made for women.

Not that we care. We're two-and-half sheets to the wind, and by the time our wine glasses are empty, we should be a full three sheets.

The muscular man on the screen grabs the "vile" woman's hair, pulls her to the bed and as he sits on the mattress drags her over his lap. His free hand slaps one ass cheek then the next. Her fake wails are so loud, I wonder if they dubbed in the slapping sounds.

"Jillian, have you ever been spanked before?" Kasie says to me, her red hair brilliant as the afternoon sunlight shines through the window.

"During hazing week to get into Sigma." Brow furrowed, I look at her. "You were there, don't you remember?"

"No, I mean by a guy. During sex."

The man on the TV has stopped spanking the woman and switched to finger fucking her while she's still on his lap. Her moans grow in volume, hardly matching the thrusts of his finger.

"No," I say softly. "You?"

She shakes her head, takes another sip. At the rate we're going, we'll be asleep before dinner.

The man on the screen has gone back to slapping the woman's ass cheeks, turning them red, so he must be actually making contact. Most women in her position would be screaming and crying by then, but she's squealing with pleasure. Maybe they anesthetized her ass before filming.

"I'm sure a lot of guys wanted to spank us," Kasie says suddenly. "We were quite the teases."

"We still are."

"Damn right!" Kasie says, and we drink to that.

She's right. Neither one of us has changed much. Other than some crow's feet and having to spend a little more time at the gym to keep the weight off, we're still the slender, pretty-faced brunette and redhead that we were back in college.

The man on the TV has pulled the woman off his lap and bent her over the bed. He enters in one quick thrust and, gripping her waist, fucks her fast and hard from the start. She groans with every jackhammering thrust.

"You ever miss those days?" I say after a bit.

"All the time," Kasie says without hesitation. "Men our age are desperate to get married. They feel like they're falling behind."

I nod. "Fuck them once and they think we're engaged."

"That was the nice thing about young studs. All they wanted to do was fuck." She sips her wine then motions with her glass toward the TV. "You know, I think *he's* the one doing some vile and foul things to her right now."

The man on the screen pulls the woman's hair back, as he rams into her. A finger on his free hand is planted firmly in her butthole. He's calling her "a dirty slut" and "my little whore," as she continues to squeal in delight.

"She deserved it," I say, and we laugh again. "I'm glad you came down for the weekend, Kasie. It's great seeing you again. I haven't laughed like this in a while."

"Me either. I'm glad we're still friends."

"Once a Sigma," I start, and she finishes our sorority's unofficial motto with me, "always a Sigma."

A leaf blower starts up, and its roar drowns out the woman's fake squeals on the TV. A young man just as muscular as the guy on the screen walks past the living room window, taking care of my patch of Ohio's fallen autumn leaves. His dirty blond hair is apparent even under his baseball cap, as are those deep, chocolate brown eyes.

Kasie perks up. "Aren't you the lucky one? Who's that?"

"I see you've noticed Max. He's quite the hunk, isn't he?"

"For sure. Have you fucked him yet?"

I laugh. "Unfortunately not. He's my best friend Aime's son."

Kasie's full lips' pouted. "That's too bad. So your pal Aime lives next door?"

"Mm-hmm. She's gone for the weekend or I'd introduce you. Max is a student over at Ohio State, runs a yard business on weekends to pay the tuition."

"This Aime is gone, you say? Maybe some of Max's friends will come over later."

I laugh. "You're insufferable."

"But satisfied. Well, most of the time…"

We giggle, as I refill her glass of wine. "You know that guy on the porn video looks a lot like Bryant from college."

Kasie leans forward. "He does now that you mention it! Do you think that's him?"

I shake my head. "Bryant's dick was a lot smaller."

Kasie focuses on the screen as the guy's cock darts in and out of the fake screaming woman. "Yeah, it was."

There's a knock on the door. I jump up, fumble for the remote, see Kasie has it.

"Quick, turn it off!" I say.

She takes her sweet time picking up the remote, and as she does, I glance at the door. It's Max, looking through the window directly at us.

"Hurry up!"

Once the TV goes off, I speed walk to the door, open it. "Max, how are you?" A rush of cold air sweeps into the house. "Come in, warm up a little."

As I pull the door fully open for him, he steps inside, rubs his gloved hands and shivers a minute. He glances toward the TV and Kasie, who's looking around the chair at him.

"Hi, I'm Kasie," she says, giving him a smile and a

little wave.

He nods to her then looks at me. "I just wanted to see if you'd given any thought to signing up for the snow removal service?" His voice possesses a deep timbre.

I don't have the heart to tell him that in this poor economy I'm cutting back on expenses, and his service is one of those I probably can do without.

As if sensing my anxiety, Kasie quick speaks up. "Come sit down, Max. Looks like you've been working hard out there and need a rest."

His face reddens a little. "It's nothing too difficult–"

Kasie gives him that same pouty face no guy in college could resist.

"Well, I suppose a few minutes wouldn't hurt."

A broad smile returns to Kasie's face, and she pats the sofa cushion next to her chair. Max makes his way toward the living room, but I grab his wrist. "Your jacket and cap."

"Oh sorry," he says, and takes them off then places them and his dirty gloves on the coat hooks next to the door. "Wouldn't want to get leaves all over your house."

He heads into the living room, wearing a keen plaid flannel shirt and tight jeans, and I admire his pert ass. He sits down on the sofa right where Kasie patted.

"Jillian tells me you're going to OSU?"

He nods. "Studying business management."

"Impressive. Looks like you're putting what you've learned into practice."

I can tell what Kasie is up to; I've seen it a dozen times in college. Trying not stumble, I head to the kitchen for another wine glass.

"Attending school while running a business – that must be stressful," I overhear Kasie say from the living room.

Then the thought crosses my mind, *Can I do this with my best friend's son?*

Well, he's an adult; he can make his own decisions. Right?

I return to the living room with the glass and pick up the almost empty bottle of wine. "Drink?" I say to Max.

"I probably shouldn't, given that I'm operating equipment."

Kasie's seductions always calls for the guy to get a little drunk. Maybe he'll save me from having to make a decision. I set down the glass and bottle on the end table.

"Tell me more about this snow removal service," Kasie says.

Max goes into a long spiel about the services he'll offer and his low rates and what he plans to do with the money, all while Kasie gazes at him, smiling, pretending to listen intently.

When he finishes, she looks past him to me, "That sounds like a great service, Jillian. You should sign up."

"Well..."

They're both staring at me, waiting for me to say *yes* – Max because he obviously wants the money, Kasie because she probably wants to see more of Max. Who wouldn't? He's always got that sexy one day-old stubble on his face.

"Well," I repeat, "I'm probably not going to be able to, Max. With the economy as it is, I need to cut back on some of my expenses. I'm sorry, I wish I could."

He momentarily frowns. "No need to apologize, I understand."

Kasie leans toward Max, taps his wrist. "Oh, you're not giving up that easily, are you?"

Max's brow furrows. "Well, she's a neighbor and friend. It wouldn't be right to pressure someone into buying something from you just because they're your neighbor and friend."

"I admire your ethics," Kasie says. "But there must some kind of...*arrangement* that could be worked out."

His lips purse in thought for a long second. "Sure, that's possible. What do you have in mind?"

I sit there not saying anything, just staring at his chocolate brown eyes. If Kasie wants to seduce him, she can, but I'm not going to. "Um, well what would you suggest, Max?" I say.

"Maybe a discounted price. Or you could pay a set amount each month so that your payments extend into spring. Or-"

Kasie touches his elbow. "Oh Max, you're thinking of an arrangement in terms of *money*. Think outside the box. There are *other* ways of payment than the dollar."

Max's brow furrows again. I slowly shake my head, mouth *no* to Kasie.

"You'll have to ask Jillian what she has in mind," she says.

Max turns to me, those brown eyes of his

questioning. Kasie slowly nods, mouths *yes* to me.

"Well, let me think about it," I say.

Max rises. "That's no problem. I better get back to the leaf blowing."

"Are you sure you don't want to stay a little longer?" Kasie says. "We were just watching a video, and you could watch it a while with us."

My eyes go wide.

"Thank you anyway," Max says. "But it'll be dark soon."

"Okay then," Kasie says. "It was nice meeting you, Max." She bats her eyes at him.

"You too," he says and heads toward the door.

Kasie raises the remote and turns on the video. The woman's long moans and the man's grunts echo through the living room, as he thrusts into her pussy, his finger still fully buried in her ass.

Max turns around, stares with big eyes at the TV.

Kasie and I look around the side of our chairs at him. Max blushes, as his eyes stay glued to the screen.

"You're not embarrassed by that are you?" Kasie nodded at the screen.

"Uh, no, I...uh, my apologies for interrupting you."

"Oh, you're not interrupting. Actually, you were about to *join* us."

"Well, the leaves *are* off the walkway and driveway." Max watches the screen the entire time he speaks.

I glance back at it. The man has finished pummeling the woman's pussy and is now working on pressing his cock into her ass. With each small push, she lets out a surprise yelp and then giggle.

Kasie speaks in her best sultry voice. "You finding this interesting?"

He gives an unconvincing shrug. His staring eyes tell the truth though. So does the hardening cock in his pants.

Kasie sits on the couch where Max had been and pats the cushion next to her. "You're welcome to watch. I bet you're wondering how it's all going to turn out."

I shoot Kasie a surprised look and mouth *stop*.

Kasie pretends like she didn't hear me. That was half the fun of being her friend – she drags you along into something you want to do but never would on your own.

"Okay," Max says, and he sits down beside Kasie, his body a little wooden, as if nervous.

Kasie looks at me. "I think Max wants something to drink."

I fill his glass, and as handing it to him, Kasie nudges her head toward the empty sofa cushion. Sitting there, I turn back to the screen.

The man has his cock about half-way in the woman's ass, and this time she is honestly feeling it, letting out grunts and groans, as she grips the sheets not so much out of pleasure but as if painfully holding on for dear life.

Kasie watches the video for a few seconds then glances at Max's lap. She grins, and I look there too. His hard-on presses his pants outward, like a long steel tube is in there.

Max notices us and pink-faced suddenly crosses his legs.

Kasie rubs his knee. "Oh, there's no need to be all embarrassed." She gently separates his crossed legs then runs a finger up his inner thigh and palms his bulge. "I wouldn't mind helping you with that."

He gazes at Kasie, as her fingers rub his cock through his jeans. He lets go a low moan.

I run a finger along my lips, find myself sucking on it. *Kasie already has taken this past the point of return,* I tell myself. *So long as he doesn't tell his mother, what happens with Sigma stays with Sigma.* I reach over and rub my hand on his chest, letting the fingers creep into the spaces between his shirt's buttons until I find skin.

Kasie undoes his jeans snap and pulls down his zipper, as my finger runs down the length of Max's torso then hooks inside his jeans and underwear and tugs at them. Kasie does the same on the other side, and Max lifts his butt so we can pull them down.

His long, thick cock bounces free.

Kasie smiles joyfully at it. "That's really fucking impressive."

Maybe it is the alcohol, maybe it is my lust, but either way I'm too far gone. "We should taste it," I say.

Kasie's head ducks into his lap, and she drags her tongue over his shaft. An instant later, she sucks on it as stroking its base with her tender fingers.

A deep moan escapes Max's mouth, and I take his chin in my hand then press my lips to his. He opens his mouth to me, and I stroke his tongue with mine.

I undo each of his shirt's buttons and kiss the revealed skin beneath, as Kasie slurps on his cock, her red hair splayed over his lap.

Once I reach the last button, Kasie comes up for air. I lean over then cup Max's balls and suck on each one. Kasie's head returns to bobbing up and down on his cock.

Max's moans of pleasure fill the room. His hand runs along my waist and caresses my ass. My pussy tingles.

Kassie pulls away from Max's cock and begins a striptease, first slinking out of her light sweater and then slowly removing the bra beneath.. Not that Max notices, for my hand takes over where Kasie's mouth left off, stroking his cock, it lined thick with her saliva. As she turns around and wiggles out of her tight jeans, his eyes close and head arches back.

When Kasie finishes undressing, I can't help myself. Her strawberry blonde patch always fires the lust inside me, and I leave Max's cock, get on all fours in front of Kasie, and run my tongue across her inner thigh. As she gasps in pleasure, my tongue finds her wet, swollen slit and darts inside.

Max must feel left out, for he gets on his knees behind me and undoes my jeans snap then tugs them downward along with my panties. I wiggle a little to help him slide them over my round ass then lift each knee in turn as he finishes pulling them over my feet.

He caresses my bare ass then gets on all fours behind me and swipes his tongue over my pussy. I gasp. When he pulls away, I wiggle my butt at him.

Kasie lays on the floor before me. I lean onto my elbows so my tongue can reach her patch, jutting my ass upward so Max can better reach it. He places both hands on my ass cheeks and spreads them until my pussy is fully exposed to him.

His tongue licks straight up my slit, separating the wet folds, and I gasp again in pleasure. Within seconds, his tongue finds my clit, and as my eyes close, my breathing deepens. He's right on target – must have had some practice with those freshmen girls at OSU – and soon my hips are gyrating into his face. One of my palms reaches back to his hand that holds my thigh, as my gasps turn into low moans that grow louder by the second.

I can't concentrate anymore on Kasie's pussy, and within seconds of me leaving it, her hand reaches up to the crown of my head and presses it to her slit. Though trying to flick my tongue against her clit, all I can do is gasp warm breath onto it, as my muscles tense.

"Right there," I manage to get out to Max. "Yes, yes, yes!"

My entire body tenses, then my hips buck into him, as I go cross-eyed with pleasure. A long second later, my body loosens, seems to half-melt onto my living room floor.

I roll next to Kasie and look up at Max, who's on his knees, his thick and long cock fully erect, as he stares down at two wet, naked pussies, probably not sure which one to fuck first.

"Did you like how I tasted?" I ask him.

He nods vigorously.

Kasie deserves a good orgasm for ensuring I got one, and I need time to rest before we get down to fucking, so I nod my head toward her. "If you liked me, then you've got to taste her strawberry shortcake pussy."

Max lays down on his tummy between her legs, places his hands on her thighs, and goes to work eating her out.

Kasie's neck arches back, and her hips slowly press into Max's face, as she lets go a low "Ohhhh."

Maybe Max's tongue is tired, for he keeps coming up for air, breaking the steady rhythm a woman needs to cum. So I get onto my tummy next to him and with a palm on the back of his head, hold it in place so he can't leave her pussy. He doesn't seem to mind, and within moments Kasie is moaning loudly.

Her entire body writhes, like it's under the spell of some witchdoctor. Max's hard body contrasts with her curves, and he remains focused on pleasing her. Watching two people make love in real life is far more exciting than watching two people act it out on TV.

Then Kasie's entire body shakes as she moans, the upper half of her body folding forward then falling back onto the carpet with a smile of intense satisfaction. When her body stops twitching, I lift my hand from Max's head.

He gets on his knees, his mouth wet from Kasie's juices, and breathing hard. "That was a nasty thing you did, holding my head down between her legs," he says to me.

I grin. "Yeah, it was *vile*. So what're you going to do about it?"

"Lay on your back," he says.

I do, and before looking up at Max, he's on his knees between my legs, gripping my ankles and pulling my legs and ass into the air. His cock slides all the way into me, not giving me a chance to get used to his length or thickness, but I'm wet enough to accommodate him. Such is the pleasure of a young buck servicing you.

My breathing grows heavy, as Max pounds into me, and then Kasie gets on all fours over me and lowers her breasts to my mouth. I lick each one, swirling my tongue toward her nipples, and soon the room is filled with the sounds of Max's grunts, Kasie's moans, and my gasps.

Kasie looks up at Max, her nipple still in my mouth. "You've been fantasizing about her for a long time, haven't you?"

Max nods, his eyes half-closed as he thrusts, somehow gets out an "Yes."

"When you were a teenager, you jerked off thinking about her, didn't you?"

He nods again. "Yes."

"How foul! Well, this is your reward for taking good care of your body. See, good things do come to those who work hard."

As Max's grip tightens on my ankles and his cock hammers me even faster, Kasie shimmies down to my pussy. Her tongue darts out, somehow finding my clit.

"Oh fuck!" I let out, as the pleasure grows even more intense.

Max pulls out of me and thrusts his cock at Kasie face. She leaves my pussy and sucks on his member again, taking it deep into her mouth. The emptiness in my pussy, the coldness on my clit, is excruciating.

Then, as if sensing I needed attention, Max's cock fills me once again, and Kasie's warm tongue returns to my clit. I'm too dizzy to know anymore where the pleasure is coming from, and my body tenses.

Then Max brings my foot to his mouth, licks my toes as thrusting into me. It's too much, and my senses spill over the edge into orgasm. As I scream out in pleasure, Max's hot cum spills into me.

A few seconds later, we separate, our bodies slick with sweat, each of us gasping for air and the TV the only sounds.

"Will you ever do foul things again?" the man says to the woman, his cum splattered across her face.

"No sir," she says demurely, then – as the camera zooms in on her – she turns to the audience and winks.

All of us laugh.

"Looks like we missed the video," Max said.

Kasie grabs the remote and shuts off the TV. "We'll have to watch it again tomorrow."

I sit up. "Since your mother is gone, Max, you're welcome to spend the night with us." I deserve a spanking for the vile and foul thing I've done, after all.

"I'd like that," he says, his cock starting to deflate, though it's large even in its natural state.

"Oh, and you can't ever tell your mother about this, understood?"

His young face grins. "Sons never talk about their sex lives to their mothers."

Why didn't I think about that? "And about the snow removal service? We were thinking this might serve as payment for it."

Max shakes his head. "That only covered half of the season."

Kasie and I look at one another wide-eyed.

"But if you want to cover the other half of the season..." He taps Kasie's chest. "Then get on your back and spread your legs."

"Sure, anything to help a friend in need," Kasie says.

She rolls over, and Max gets on his knees between her legs and lifts them in the air as his now erect cock aims for her pussy.

She smirks. "Plow me, baby, plow me."

The Roomie

It's freezing, but I'll wait. I'm outside the building where Keenan has class, the building where I last saw him, where we kissed before he ran off to his lecture, and I made the long drive back to Central College, halfway across the state. I imagine the surprised look on his face, then it breaking into an excited smile, as he rushes to me and takes me in his arms. We kiss, and suddenly the pelting sleet melts away in his warmth, as he lifts me in the air, and spins me around, my pony tail swinging behind me like some moon tethered to a planet.

I stuff my hands into my pea coat's pockets, just a minute or so more. The cold wind blowing between the canyon of buildings stings. Students begin filing out of the building, and my eyes go on high alert, watching for him.

He does not come out.

Do I have the wrong building? The wrong class time? Did he go out a different exit?

I wait. Soon I am standing alone in a cold Michigan winter breeze, hands still stuffed in pocket. The building is right, the time is right, I remember it well the last time I was here. Keenan is not one for change; if he entered this door, he'll come out it.

Then the campus carillon plays in the distance, marking the top of the hour. A new class has begun, and still no Keenan. He must be talking to a professor.

Five minutes pass. I resist the urge to text him; this visit is going to be a surprise.

He doesn't have class after this, so maybe I missed him in the crowd, and he went back to his dorm room. Maybe he's ill, didn't even go to class. There could be a thousand other reasons.

Marching head down into the cold wind, I go to his dorm. For a moment, I think I see him walking in the distance, but it can't be him, for the guy and a blonde co-ed are holding hands. Weird how the mind plays tricks on you when longing for someone.

***

I knock on Keenan's door. My feet feel frozen from the walk through the cold.

The door opens, and there stands his roomie, Noah. His eyes – pale blue like a robin's egg –widen when he sees it's me.

"Jocelyn! Come in," he says. "What're you doing here?"

"I wanted to surprise Keenan." I follow him into their dorm room. "But he didn't come out of his hall where he has class. Do you know where he is?"

Noah runs a hand through his sandy blond hair and looks down at the tile floor. "Yeah, I don't know when Keenan is getting back."

"That wasn't my question. I asked if you knew where he is?"

He hesitates. "Actually no."

Something's wrong, I can feel it. I glance around the room. There's no picture of me on Keenan's desk.

"Is something going on?" I ask.

Noah's handsome jaw twists to a side. "Jocelyn, I really don't want to get mixed up in all this."

"Then something *is* going on."

He says nothing for a moment, picks up a dirty shirt from the floor and with his well-muscled arms tosses it in the hamper at the other end of the room. "Jocelyn, sit down."

I pull out the chair to Keenan's desk and take a seat, as Noah turns his own toward me then sits. "I always want to be honest with you, Jocelyn, but I also have to live with Keenan until the end of the semester."

My eyes narrow. "What are you not telling me?"

"Joceyln, Keenan has been seeing someone behind your back."

My mouth drops. Noah always has been a little sweet on me, but why would he say that about Keenan? The two of us have been dating three years now, since high school. "You must be mistaken," I finally say.

"I wish I were–"

"You're just saying this because you've always wanted to go out with me! Some friend you are to Keenan."

Noah holds his hands up. "Jocelyn – yes, I have always found you attractive, but I never would do something like that. You and Keenan are my friends."

I rise quickly. "Yeah, well when I see Keenan, you can

damn well expect me to tell him what you tried." I march for the door.

"Jocelyn–"

Before he can finish, a slammed door separates the two of us.

***

My fuming has left me hot, but even that is not enough to keep me warm in Michigan's January chill. Why would Noah say that about Keenan? I head to the student center to think. Keenan usually eats lunch there at noon, and I can catch up with him then.

The student center's dim light temporarily blinds me as I step in from the snow-covered grounds and white-clouded sky. I find a table a ways from the entrance and plop into a chair.

And then my mouth falls open...again.

There's Keenan, sitting on the other side of the center, with a blonde. They're making googly eyes at one another, laughing and giggling.

I'm sure it's the same woman I saw holding hands with the guy I mistook for Keenan while on my way to his dorm room.

And then I want to cover my eyes.

Keenan's hand is under the table, caressing her thigh.

***

Noah opens the door. "Joceyln, thank you for coming back–"

I barge in the past room him, and he closes the door. "Noah, I owe you an apology." I gaze out the window at the bare trees.

114

"It's okay, Joceyln. I understand. I'd think the same thing if someone said that me."

I turn around, desperately trying not to cry. "I saw them, Noah. In the student center. Flirting with one another. His hand was on her thigh. And I saw them earlier – except I wasn't sure it was him – and he was holding the same woman's hand. Noah, you were right!"

The dam bursts, and tears pour down my face.

Noah takes me into his arms. "Oh Joceyln, I'm so sorry."

I press my head into Noah's broad chest, his shirt collecting my tears, as I let it all out. His arms feel so warm, so reassuring.

"How could he do this to me?" I say, pulling away. "How long has this been going on, Noah?"

He hands me a tissue from his desk. "About two or three weeks."

"I'm going to break up with him," I say. "Can I stay here until he gets back? I want him to look me in the eyes and see just how much he's hurt me."

Noah nods. "I don't want to be here when you two have your…talk."

"I understand. And Noah – don't worry…I won't tell him that you told me about his affair."

He says nothing for a moment. "I appreciate that. I need to get to class. But you're welcome to stay here. I should be back in an hour."

"Okay," I say as sniffling. "I'll see you in an hour."

Noah pulls on his navy pea coat then grabs his book pack. A moment later, I'm left in the silent dorm room.

My face falls into my hands as I cry again.

***

After 20 minutes or so, I run out of tears. I use Noah's towel to dry my face. His scent, a comforting sandalwood, lingers on the towel, and I breathe it in.

I decide to snoop around.

In Keenan's desk drawer is a picture of the blonde. Beneath it is mine. I find a couple of love notes from her to him, and simmering decide not to read them for fear I'll start throwing stuff around. Next, I rifle through Keenan's closet, find a strand of gold hair on one of his sweaters. I crumple to the floor, find the tears for a short cry.

As I wipe them away with the back of my hand, I rise, decide to check Keenan's laptop on his desk. I don't know why. A glutton for punishment, I guess.

Raising the screen, I hit the power switch. A couple of moments later, it asks for a PIN number. Keenan always used his birth year for his passwords, so I type it, and up pops his desktop.

It's full of MP4 files, each named with a single word – *blonde, redhead, brunette, brownies, tinytits, blowjob, anal, spanking* …

I click one. A porno plays.

What the fuck?

***

Shutting down his laptop, my hands roll into fists. Not only is my so-called boyfriend cheating on me, he's addicted to porn.

Not that I have anything against watching an erotic

video from time to time with your lover. But dozens of them kept on his laptop? Is he rewatching them?

I pace back and forth across the dorm room floor, wonder if I can even confront Keenan now. I'm so angry, I don't know what I might do to him.

And then exhaustion takes over. It's been all too much. I collapse onto Noah's bed and curl up. His pillow smells slightly sweet and earthy, like his towel. I dab my eyes and fall asleep.

***

I wake to a dark room, except for a small lamp lit in the corner. Noah's blanket is on me.

"Good evening, sleepyhead," Noah says from Keenan's desk. He closes his textbook.

"What time is it?"

"Nearly seven. Hungry?"

I nod as sitting up, his blanket slipping from my shoulders to my lap. "Sorry – I didn't meant to fall asleep. Has Keenan been here?"

Noah shakes his head.

"Did you put the blanket on me?"

"You looked cold."

I give him a small smile. "That was sweet of you. Yeah, I'm a little hungry."

"I'll order a pizza for us. Just tomato and onions on your half?"

He remembers. "Sounds perfect."

"I trust you're all rested now."

"So much happened earlier today that I felt drained. I was so angry. I *still* am."

Noah whips out his phone and starts tapping away. "Don't worry about it. I understand. ... Pizza should be here in 20 minutes."

I stand up and stretch. He watches me.

We make small talk until the pizza arrives. Usually I'm not one for superficialities, but I sense Noah is trying to keep my mind off Keenan. I appreciate that.

As we eat, Noah's phone buzzes. He checks it and grimaces. "Oh Jesus, I can't believe what he's asking."

"Something wrong?"

"Keenan texted me."

My blood boils. "What did he say?"

"I'll let you read it." He hands me his phone.

Am staying night at Taylor's. If Jocelyn calls, cover 4 me?

"That fucking bastard!" I shout.

"I've never 'covered' for him before, Joceyln. I swear!"

Handing him back his phone, I've suddenly lost my appetite. "Don't worry, I believe you. You have a beer to go with this pizza? I could use one right now."

Noah gets me a bottle from his mini-fridge. "You promise not to throw it at me?"

"Promise. But if Keenan comes through that door, you better duck."

He grins, pops off the bottle cap, and hands me the beer.

I take a long draught of it. "Did you know that Keenan is into porn?"

He shrugs. "Every guy on the floor watches it some time."

"No, I mean *really* into it. I looked on his laptop – he's got dozens of porn videos on his desktop."

Noah's face blanches. "No...I didn't know that. He doesn't watch when I'm around."

"Maybe we should check one out. Just to see what he's watching."

"You sure that's a good idea?"

"I'm curious. Aren't you?"

He shrugs. "Sure."

"Sure" as in "Yes, I'm curious too" or "Sure" as in "Yes, let's watch one"? There isn't much of a leap between the two. So I power up Keenan's desktop and log in. I click the video titled *Spanking.* It's something Keenan often tries to get me to do with him, but I always refuse. I wonder what he finds so exciting about it.

The video opens with a distraught woman sitting in what looks to be the back room of some store. A guy wearing a badge with handcuffs in his back pocket comes in, tells her she's in big trouble. She denies doing anything wrong. He tells her they have her on video shoplifting. However, since she gave up that item, if she's willing to cooperate, he's willing to forget calling the police since this is her first offense. She asks what she has to do.

He tells her he first needs to make sure that she hasn't stolen anything else, so he needs to conduct a strip search. She balks, but then he reminds her that if she refuses, he'll just call the police and file the report with them. She relents.

Jesus Christ, who writes this crap?

He has her lean against a table then pats down her naked body, and she starts to get turned on. A moment later, he's pulling apart her ass cheeks, telling her he needs to make sure she didn't try to hide anything there. When he's done, she asks if she can go.

He says he's not done and slaps each of her ass cheeks. She asks him what he's doing, and he says he's trying to shake loose anything she might have shoved up her ass. Claiming again that she didn't put anything there, he says they'll find out in a few minutes, and continues to spank her.

Keenan is into this idiotic nonsense?

Well, I do have to admit that the sound of his hand smacking her bare bottom is kind of hot.

After ten minutes of spanking in which he leaves her ass cherry red, he tells her to bend over the table. "You said I could go when you were done checking," she protests, but he says he's not done checking, that she could have put something in her pussy.

"After checking that, then I can go?" she says.

"Yes," he responds.

She bends over, and he unzips his pants and drops them along with his boxer. The biggest goddamn cock I've ever seen – it must be eight inches long and as wide as my wrist – pops out, fully erect. He takes her hips and in one thrust is in her, fucking her harder with each passing second.

And she's enjoying it, of course.

Mhm, his grunts and groans are kind of a turn on.

I glance at Noah, and his eyes are glued to the laptop

screen. My eyes dip down to his lap. He's hard as a rock, if the bulge there is to be believed.

At last the guy in the video pulls out of her and grabbing the woman's hair, brings her to her knees in front of him. He strokes his cock with one hand, groaning the entire time, then spurts all over her face.

She smiles and licks some of the cum off her lips.

"Your pussy is clear. I don't expect to ever see you in here again, got it?" he says and lets go of her hair.

"I promise," she says, but you know she probably will be, just so she can enjoy his search.

The video comes to an end.

I glance again at Noah's bulge. "Want another beer?" I say.

"Yeah, that would be great," he says, almost as if he's out of breath.

I grin then get two bottles, one for each of us.

"Thanks," he says.

I tip my bottle toward his lap. "Figured you didn't want to be embarrassed."

That turns his face red. "And you didn't find that hot?" he says.

"Parts of it I did. Want to watch another one?"

"If you do."

I click on the one called *spanking2*. It's similar to the first one we watched.

As the man in the video smacks the butt of the woman over his knees, I say to Noah, "Have you ever spanked a woman before?"

He shakes his head.

"Would you like to?"

"If she's willing."

I rise, stop the video, and turning to him pull the hair tie from my head then shake my mane loose so it falls about my shoulders. "Look Noah, I know that you like me."

"I've always thought how lucky Keenan was to have a girlfriend like you."

Leaning forward, close to his face, I slowly run a finger across his lips. "And I've always thought you were one delicious, looking guy. Now you can have the woman that Keenan was so lucky to call his."

His large hand caresses my upper arm. "Joceyln...is it wise to do this after all that has happened to you today?"

I bring a finger to his mouth and shush him. "I want this, Noah. In fact, I've wanted you for a long time."

Neither one is a lie.

Our lips meet, and I breathe in his sandalwood scent, woodsy and creamy all at the same time. His mouth moves along my chin to my neck then down to that sweet spot where it meets the shoulder. I let go a low moan as my eyes close.

Sliding onto his lap, we kiss again, as our hands slip under one another's shirts. I feel the hard plates of his muscles along his stomach as his fingers trail up my waist then find my breasts. I rub my crotch against his bulge, and his hips rise, as if trying to enter me, but our clothing is in the way.

Besides, I have something else in mind than a quick

fuck.

I slide off his lap, pull my blouse over my head then loosen my bra, let gravity take it to the tile floor. He gazes at my two globes.

"I'd like to try something, if you don't mind." My fingers undo my jeans' snap, and I wiggle them down my legs.

"What's that?"

"Would you spank me?"

"Do you think you deserve one? That you're the reason Keenan is cheating on you?"

I shake my head as slipping off my shoes and socks then stepping out of the jeans puddled at my ankles. "I've never been spanked by a lover before. Watching it was kind of a turn on. I'd like to experience it."

I want to let you do something I'd never let Keenan do to me. That will be my revenge on him, to let another man – a better man than him – have that pleasure.

"Okay," he says.

I slip off my panties, notice there's a small wet spot on their front. Did that come from the video or rubbing Noah's lap?

Stepping next to him, I hope he can smell my sex. "How would you like to begin?

Noah's eyes took in my body then his hand reached out. "Like *this*."

He grabs my wrist and with a hard tug, pulls my arm so that with a squeal I fall across his lap, my butt fully exposed to him. His hand caresses my legs just below my ass, and my eyes close, luxuriating in his gentleness.

Slap!

His hand quick strikes my butt cheeks, and I wince. There is a little sting, but it doesn't last long. I feel his eyes admiring my ass as the red print of his palm upon it disappears.

Then his hand goes back to caressing my legs, and I coo. My body relaxes.

Slap!

I let out a tiny yelp.

Slap!

He strikes the other cheek, harder than before, and I moan.

Moan?

No, I can't be enjoying this, I think to myself.

Slap!

My pussy grows wetter. Surely he can feel it, even through his pants.

Slap! Slap!

He strikes both butt cheeks in quick succession, and I let go an "Ooh!"

Noah massages the redness of my butt, as his free hand wraps my long hair around his fist.

Slap!

When his hand hits my ass, he pulls back on the hair, bringing my head up and back. My calves rise in the air.

Slap!

"Uhhn!" My nipples, pressed against his leg, harden.

He massages my ass again, leaving me to suffer with anticipation.

Then…*Slap! Slap! Slap! Slap! Slap!*

His hand hits hard in quick, successive strikes against each butt cheek, and I gasp. My hips grind against his leg.

"Oh, that feels so fucking good," I whimper.

His hand comes down once more upon my bare bottom, then again and again, and I moan as the burn rises from my ass and desire swirls from my sopping pussy. Its lips stretch wide against his leg, my exposed clit finds the fabric of his pants, and I grind, as he keeps slapping my ass.

I alternately gasp and moan, as every muscle in my body tenses. And then I spasm, cumming right there while over his knees.

***

After a few minutes, as I return to Earth, Noah says, "Now I'd like to try something, if you don't mind."

"Anyone who can make me cum like that doesn't need to ask my permission to try something."

Noah helps me off his knees to a standing position, though I'm a bit wobbly, then in one smooth motion he rises as lifting me. I squeal again in surprise at his strength. He tosses me onto his bed.

"Whee!" I say, as he undresses.

First he pulls his shirt over his head, and I marvel at his six-pack and those perfect pecs on his broad chest. Then his jeans – where there is a wet spot with my juices on his thigh, I notice – come off along with this shoes and socks. I admire his bulge beneath the boxers, then he takes them off.

I gulp.

Okay, it's not as big as the guy in the first video but damn near. I'd guess it was seven inches long and almost three inches around.

I bite my lower lip and grin. "So what is it you'd like to try?"

Noah doesn't answer, just takes hold of my ankles and pulls me so my pussy is at the bed's edge. He holds his cock and inserts the head into me then pulls it out and inserts it again. Each time I gasp.

The third time it stays in, and he thrusts steadily. My eyes close, and I yelp with each push.

His hand wraps around the side of my neck, and he brings me up for a kiss as fucking me. My hands grasp the sheets to balance myself, as my legs wrap around his back.

When we withdraw from our kiss and stare into one another's eyes, our hips doing all of the work, he says, "I want you to cum without me touching your clit."

A vaginal orgasm? That's pretty rare for–

He interrupts my thoughts with a long kiss, and our tongues entwine. Somehow he goes deeper into me than Keenan ever did, fills me like Keenan never could. And most important of all, he lasts longer than Keenan.

Noah's speed picks up, and I squeal with each thrust.

And then from somewhere deep inside me I feel pleasure gently lapping outward. Each time Noah fills and expands me, the more powerful those laps are and the farther out they spread. Every muscle in my body tenses again, and as Noah grunts with one last slam into me, filling me with his cum, my vaginal walls contract around his cock, those rough, lapping waves touch every part of my body, and I scream in joy.

***

I wake up the next morning in Noah's arms, the first light of the rising sun peaking at the edges of his dorm window's curtains. My body feels so warm, so relaxed spooned next to his.

"Hmm," he murmurs, as I start to wiggle away and rise. It's the last thing I want to do.

"I need to get back," I tell him. "I have three classes today and a two-hour drive ahead of me."

He sits, caresses my shoulders. "What about Keenan?"

"Give me a second."

I get up, pull my phone from my jeans and return to bed. I sense Noah's eyes watching my ass on the way there and my breasts on the way back. I type a text to Keenan: *I never want to see you again. Enjoy your life with blondie.* The depths of one's hate can run as deep as one's love.

"That's done. I just broke up with him."

Noah kisses my shoulder. "I'll miss you."

"Call me tonight." I get up and dress. He continues to watch me, his pale blue eyes filled with love.

We kiss goodbye. His sandalwood scent swirls around me, and I so want to take off my clothes and crawl back into bed with him. But I need to get back.

Just before opening the door, I turn back to him. "This weekend, come visit me at Central." I blow him a kiss on the fingertips. "I'm *not* waiting to get over Keenan."

If you got a little excited from reading this book, please take a few moments to write a review of it:
amazon.com/dp/1948872897
XOXOXO – Emily

Interview with Emily

Q: How did you start writing erotica?
A: While studying literature, I read Audre Lorde's "Uses of the Erotic: The Erotic as Power." The essays opened up a whole new world of thought for me. I decided to explore her ideas by writing erotica.

Q: Were you a fan of erotic literature before you started writing it?
A: I was. The sensuality of the writing drew me to it. Good erotica explored characters and themes that other good writing was missing.

Q: What drew you to erotica as a reader?
A: Curiosity in the salacious, lol. But I found the tales I most liked were less about the act of sex than the "why" of sex, that is the moments leading up to it.

Q: Where do you find your inspiration for erotica?
A: I create characters with problems that they need to resolve, and the sex is a metaphor for how they can best resolve it to become whole again. Coming up with problems is the easy part!

Q: Are some of the scenarios and scenes from your books real? Have you lived out some of them?
A: Some of them are real, but I never tell which ones are, lol.

Q: Do your characters ever want to take over the story?
A: All the time! Characters can take on a life of their own, and sometimes when you put them in situations,

to be true to themselves they have to get out of them in ways you the author hadn't planned.

Q: What are your favorite writing quirks?

A: I need a hot cup of coffee to my left and everyone out of the room – though for coffee shops and other public places the latter is not the case, maybe because we're all minding our own business.

Q: Any tips on writing erotica?

A: Learn the crafts of writing and storytelling. Know the difference between erotica and porn.

Q: At this point in your career, you've focused on short stories. Do you have any plans to write a novel?

A: I have 10 novels in various stages of completion. I just prefer to write short stories; I like their compactness.

Q: Do you use multiple pen names? It's a common strategy to use a different name for each kink.

A: I just use the one name "Emily Rooks." I want to make that name a brand rather than have several "brands" to handle.

Q: What's your favorite part of a man's body?

A: That's a "loaded" question, isn't it? It's the whole package really. A brain has to come with a fit body.

Q: Do you remember the first story you ever read and the impact it had on you?

A: The first story I ever read to myself was "Green Eggs and Ham" in first grade. I couldn't believe what an incredible, vast universe this new skill of reading opened to me!

About Emily Rooks

Emily Rooks is the author of erotic romance that sizzles with passion and tension. Her stories explore sexuality from a woman's perspective and feature strong female protagonists. She holds a bachelor's degree in literature and creative writing and resides in Los Angeles.

True Lust Titles

Anthologies
- Backdoor Tales
- Spanking Tales
- Spanking Tales, Volume II
- Young Studs

Short Stort Standalones
- Atonement
- Chalk
- Opportunity
- Star Pupil
- Supergirl
- Venus Fly Trap

Better Sex Guidebooks
- Essential Foreplay Tips

Connect with Emily

BlueSky
emilyrookstruelust.bsky.social

Facebook
(limited posts)
facebook.com/EmilyRooksTrueLust

Goodreads
goodreads.com/user/show/146421357-emily-rooks

Literotica
literotica.com/authors/EmilyRooks/works/stories

Pinterest
pinterest.com/emilyrookstruelust

Website
emilyrookstruelust.com

X/Twitter
x.com/EmilyRooksTrueL